# TROPICAL MADNESS

Paediatrician Serena Blake's idea of adventure is applying for a new hospital job in Dorset. Then her brother introduces her to the ruggedly handsome journalist and adventurer Jake Andrews, and she finds herself agreeing to accompany him to the African jungle in order to help sick and injured children. Soon the pair find themselves in the middle of an impending coup. And to make matters worse, Serena discovers that she's falling in love with Jake, though she's sure he will forget about her once — and *if* — they get back home . . .

NORA FOUNTAIN

# TROPICAL MADNESS

*Complete and Unabridged*

## LINFORD
*Leicester*

First published in Great Britain in 2015

First Linford Edition
published 2016

A catalogue record for this book is available
from the British Library.

ISBN 978–1–4448–2982–2

Published by
F. A. Thorpe (Publishing)
Anstey, Leicestershire

Set by Words & Graphics Ltd.
Anstey, Leicestershire
Printed and bound in Great Britain by
T. J. International Ltd., Padstow, Cornwall

This book is printed on acid-free paper

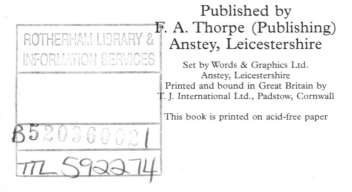

# 1

'So this is the famous Joe's Bar!'

Joe's Bar was the favourite watering hole of Serena's brother Chris and his colleagues. Working at the nearby television station, Chris co-produced a popular prime-time news programme. He took Serena's elbow now and propelled her into the softly lit but noisy interior.

'It is indeed, sis, and there's the man we've come to meet.'

Serena stopped so abruptly that Chris almost cannoned into her. 'What are you talking about, Chris? I thought you and I were going to have a quiet drink and catch up on family news — just the two of us.'

'That, too, of course.'

Serena hadn't identified the man in question, but she fervently wished she hadn't agreed to come. This wasn't her kind of place at all. It was just that she saw so little of her brother these days, so she'd accepted his invitation without question. Truth to tell, she had little time or inclination for drinking and socialising. Her job as locum in the accident and emergency department of a busy London hospital took care of that. Looking back, she often wondered how she had got through the days, let alone the nights, when she had been on call twenty-four hours a day.

Recently she had taken time out doing relief work in Africa while waiting to see if she would get the post she had applied for as a paediatrician at a Dorset hospital. The location, on the edge of Bournemouth and close to the New Forest, would suit her very well, and the doctors on the team she'd be working with if she got the post had been very friendly at the interview.

They headed for the bar, where two men at one end were talking business or something serious that required dramatic gestures, while at the other a young couple were wrapped up in each other to the exclusion of all else. That left the man sitting alone in the middle. He looked too large for the bar stool he had perched on. Standing up, he would be tall. Thick black hair curled over the collar of the white shirt he was wearing, which was unbuttoned at the neck without a tie; Serena could see through the mirror behind the bar. His face was obscured by an array of colourful bottles. His stance was tough and uncompromising; she gleaned that much from the broad shoulders and long, rangy body. Though still, there was an alertness and vitality about him, and for an instant she wondered what his face was like. She felt a tiny spark of interest as she conjured one to match the rest of him, which she suppressed at once.

He moved, their eyes met in the mirror, and he swivelled round. Serena found herself speared by hooded green eyes that raked her from head to toe, taking in the pleated cream top that skimmed her curvy body and the matching culottes that accentuated her slender hips and long legs, before coming to rest on her glamorous stilettos. At work, she went in for low-heeled comfort, keeping killer heels for rare social occasions. Now, as she experienced an unwelcome heat under that knowing gaze, she wished she'd worn trainers.

At last the wretched man's gaze moved to Chris. 'Ah, there you are,' he said to her brother. 'Are you two together? I thought we were here to discuss business. Looks like it could be pleasure, too.'

While the two men greeted each other, Serena discreetly continued to scrutinise Chris's friend: in his mid-thirties, and attractive in a rugged rather than conventional way, he had a wonderful bone structure and jet-lashed eyes. He also exuded confidence and virility. He was the sort of man Serena avoided like the plague.

'It's both, I hope,' said Chris.

'Serena, this is Jake. Jake, my sister, Serena.'

'Your sister?' No need for him to look so pleased. He wasn't the first man to look at her wide blue eyes and silver-blond hair, tonight coiled in a classic chignon, and see her as a plaything. He slid off his stool, and she saw that he was as tall as she had surmised; intimidatingly so. She added a layer of frost to her expression.

'Are you in the business, Serena?' he asked her. 'An actress, maybe? Or a presenter on one of those breakfast shows I always manage to miss?'

'How do you do, Jake — and no, I'm not,' she replied icily.

'That's a nice tan you have.' He ignored her rebuff. 'Unusual with such fair colouring. It is natural, I take it?'

'I've been away,' she volunteered; and, aware of Chris scowling, she added, 'You look pretty brown yourself.'

'I've been away, too. I have a little place in Provence where I escape whenever I can.'

'How nice!' She knew she sounded trite; stupid, even.

'I suppose you recognise Jake?' said Chris.

'Should I?'

'Television journalist, darling of the gossip columnists, and more recently, successful author.'

'Sorry, I seldom watch television — just the odd drama or documentary,' she confessed. 'I get the news on my car radio when I'm out and about. I recognise some of the faces here, though; mostly actors.' Several of whom, she noted, exchanged greetings with Jake.

Chris grunted. 'Let's sit down,' he said, bagging a newly vacated table.

'You could be treading on my ego,' Jake murmured, pulling out a chair for her.

Serena glanced up, pleased to find he was smiling, a broad slash of white creasing his face and lighting his quite beautiful eyes.

'Sor — '

'Please don't apologise again,' he cut in. 'I wish more people were like you — not recognising me, I mean. I hardly dare to go out till after dark.'

'Scotch and soda for me,' Chris ordered when he got the barman's attention. 'A refill for Jake — and white wine for you, Serena?' She nodded.

'I'll get these,' Jake insisted when the drinks arrived.

'How did you find the Horn then, sis?' Chris asked as Jake dealt with the barman.

'I didn't. I left that to the pilot.'

'Very funny! You didn't fall for some personable young medic out there?'

'Don't be absurd. We were far too busy dealing with sick and starving refugees to find time for romance.'

'You can't carry a torch for Robbie forever.'

'Leave it,' she replied sharply as Jake turned to hand her a drink.

'Sorry, love. I'll go and see if our table's ready. Shan't be a tick.'

Serena watched her brother's familiar relaxed gait as he strolled away, his blond hair — as fair as her own — catching the light.

'Who's Robbie?' a deep voice enquired in her ear.

'He was my fiancé. He's dead,' she stated baldly.

She caught a whiff of expensive aftershave and a clean, elusive maleness as Jake leaned towards her. 'I'm sorry,' he said, taking a mouthful of Scotch before setting his glass down. He was leaning too close and Serena's stomach muscles quivered alarmingly. She wasn't in the market for a man, let alone a testosterone-packed example like Jake, so she was more than pleased when Chris rejoined them.

'Come on, folks. Our table's ready,' Chris announced.

As they ate, Serena learned that Jake's career as a television journalist had taken him to most of the warring hotspots of the world. 'Where have you been recently?' she enquired, skilfully dissecting her trout.

'Well, I'm sort of semi-retired,' he replied, spearing a succulent piece of steak while shooting Chris an odd glance.

'Jake now writes pacey best-selling novels, drawing on his experience as a journalist. He also still does the occasional documentary for us.'

'Like the one centring on the trip to central Africa your brother's proposing,' Jake chimed in.

'Central Africa? I've worked in — '

'Yes,' Chris cut her off. 'To Wadumba, east of Nigeria, to be precise. We've heard rumours of an impending coup. Jake's been out there before and knows the terrain and some of the inhabitants.'

'You want Jake to go out there to face whatever dangers — '

'In a word, yes. We got a frantic phone call at the TV station from a priest Jake knows — he's attached to a mission out there. The line went dead, unfortunately, before we finished the call.'

'What did he say, before you were cut off?' asked Serena, liking the idea of Jake taking off to face unknown dangers less and less.

'Father O'Leary said that most of his staff, comprising a young doctor and several nuns working as nurses, had taken off in fright. It left the old priest alone with one elderly nun and three patients, all young boys of around ten to twelve years of age, and all unable to be moved.'

'What kind of health issues do they have?'

'One has leukaemia — he's not expected to survive. Another has a broken leg and is not yet able to be moved. The third has a septic bite and desperately needs antibiotics. Unfortunately, the dispensary has been broken into and looted.'

'It sounds pretty grim. What kind of bite are we talking about? Mosquito? Tsetse?'

'Nothing so trivial, I'm afraid. There's a wounded lioness on the loose, too weak to hunt but not above lying in wait for any unwary villager to provide her next meal. The boy's lucky to be alive — his father died trying to save him; his uncle was badly injured.'

'That's appalling! And you want Jake to go out there to get a story, to improve your ratings?'

'Ostensibly to do a documentary,' Chris agreed equably. 'We actually want him to launch a rescue mission.'

'But as I've explained to Chris, apart from the two-man camera crew, I'd need to give the operation some authenticity,' Jake explained. 'I'd need a doctor to get those kids out safely.'

Serena felt prickles of awareness and a growing anger even before Chris spoke.

'Which is where Serena comes in,' her brother said.

'I beg your pardon?' Jake said.

'Oh, didn't I say? Serena's a doctor. She finished training as a paediatrician before volunteering for the Horn.'

'The Horn of Africa?' Jake glowered at her accusingly. 'You didn't say you'd worked in Africa.'

'Why would I? I don't see that it's any of your concern.'

'You let me think you'd been travelling and maybe got your tan sunning yourself in the Med.'

'I didn't . . . This is ridiculous!'

'The job in Dorset, if she gets it, won't start for three months,' Chris went on, undeterred. 'What could be more propitious?'

Of all the lousy tricks! Serena fumed. It wasn't the first time Chris had put her on the spot. He'd sell his own grandmother for a story. Yet how could she refuse to help those children? And then again, how could she go on a foray into the unknown with Jake Andrews? The very thought sent shivers of alarm round her system.

'No!' She may have been screaming the objection inside, but it was Jake who had voiced it aloud.

'What do you mean, no?' asked Chris. 'Jake, time is of the essence. I've booked tickets for tomorrow's late-morning flight. I want you to get in quick and get out before they know what's hit them.'

'The answer's no. I'll go myself, sure, but I'm not taking a living Barbie doll.'

Serena saw red at that. 'Now just a minute, *Mr* Andrews! If those kids need medical help and I'm prepared to go — ' which she wasn't — with him, anyway, ' — who the hell are you to try and stop me?'

'I'm not taking you, lady, and that's final!'

'Ahem!' The waiter cleared his throat politely as he took in the exchange.

'Cheese and biscuits for me,' Chris ordered nonchalantly, confident he could rescue the situation.

'A large brandy,' demanded Jake.

'Nothing for me,' said Serena. 'Thanks,' she added — it wasn't the poor waiter's fault, after all. She stood up with such force that the startled waiter only just managed to catch her chair before it fell. She marched out, ignoring her brother's pleas, collected her jacket and left.

It was late July, but night had fallen and there were shadowy areas between the streetlamps. A fine drizzle began to fall, pedestrians were few and far between, and there was not a taxi in sight. Serena knew the sensible thing to do would be return to the hotel and ask the doorman to call a cab, but there was no way she was going back there to her infuriating brother and the chauvinistic Jake Andrews. A Barbie doll indeed!

So, instead of doing the wise thing, Serena walked on briskly to where the road ahead intersected with a well-lit thoroughfare busy with traffic and pedestrians wielding umbrellas. The occasional taxi could be seen cruising along, its light showing it was free. Just a couple of hundred yards to safety.

Two scruffy young individuals were sauntering towards her along the deserted pavement. Serena took care to avoid eye contact, but she could sense their eyes on her and was aware of the threat they posed. She veered towards the pavement edge, intending to cross the street. As bad luck would have it, cars were parked there bumper to bumper, not an inch between them. She dithered a second too long and the men pounced.

Thanking the powers that be for her lessons in self-defence, she grasped the arm of the first assailant to lunge at her. Instead of resisting, she used his impetus to pull him forwards, hooked her ankle round his and sent him sprawling. He landed in a stunned heap. Had he been alone, she could have escaped.

'You wanna play games?' drawled the second man, seizing her from behind as the first man stumbled to his feet. She felt sick with fear and outrage.

Suddenly, she could hear running feet. A third attacker? Couldn't they just grab her handbag and go? Then she was free — there was the thwack of a fist connecting with flesh and bone, and the second assailant collapsed with a groan. The first, now recovered, pulled his friend up and together they hobbled off, cursing. Serena turned to thank her rescuer and came face to face with Jake Andrews.

'You!'

'Are you all right?'

'I'm fine.' She thought she was, but at that moment delayed shock hit her and she started to tremble.

'No, you're not.' His voice was gentle as he put an arm round her and pulled her close. She didn't pull away but allowed him to cushion her head against his broad chest, his arm firmly encircling her. His heart was beating a staccato rhythm and she discerned a tangy aftershave, and the clean warmth of his body. 'Better?' he asked softly.

'Yes,' she muttered and reluctantly drew away.

An empty taxi appeared and halted at Jake's command. They climbed inside.

'Your address?' Jake asked. Serena told him and he relayed her answer to the driver. 'Will there be someone there to look after you?'

Her flatmate, Debbie, would probably be there; but so, too, would Simon, Debbie's latest boyfriend, who was keen to move in. 'I expect my flatmate's there,' she said.

'I'll see you inside.' Jake paid off the driver and followed Serena into the building and up the stairs to the first-floor flat. Sure enough, Simon was in the sitting room, wearing boxer shorts and nothing else, and pouring wine into two glasses.

'Serena!' he greeted mockingly, and then caught sight of Jake. 'Good heavens, little Miss Icicle's got a playmate.' He gestured to the couch in an 'it's all yours' gesture before heading for Debbie's room. Serena prayed that Jake hadn't heard Simon's sarcasm, but he clearly had.

'Who the hell was that?' he demanded.

'That's Simon, Debbie's boyfriend.'

'What did he mean, 'little Miss Icicle'? Has he been trying it on with you?'

'Please!'

'In other words, he has — and you've had to slap him down.'

'He's my flatmate's boyfriend, so it's doubly awkward and doubly offensive. I absolutely can't stand him.'

'Do you hate men in general? Maybe you think Robbie let you down by dying?'

'Don't be absurd.' Yet there was a grain of truth in what he said. He was far too perceptive. 'I'm happy as I am. I just wish people would leave me alone.'

'You're still in shock,' he said, changing the subject. 'How about a coffee?'

'I'll make some.'

He followed her into the kitchen, where she set the coffee machine going and prepared a tray, ignoring the debris of Debbie's intimate dinner. A quick shake revealed an empty biscuit tin.

'Damn, they've eaten my chocolate chip cookies.'

'So? What's a packet of biscuits?'

'It so happens I made them.'

'Oh, I see. My favourites, too. I'm beginning to share your dislike.'

Serena glanced up to receive another of those devastating smiles. She smiled back.

'That's better,' Jake said. 'I was beginning to wonder if you ever smiled.'

Not often, she suddenly realised, except at work. Young patients responded well to a cheerful smile. 'You have a point,' she conceded. She poured two mugs of coffee and added them to the tray together with milk and sugar.

'Let me take that.' He carried the tray through and set it on a low table in front of the settee.

'Help yourself to milk and sugar,' Serena said.

'I take it black.'

She took a sip from her mug. 'I haven't thanked you for rescuing me.'

'That's true,' he agreed.

'So I'm thanking you now,' she told him pointedly, and he grinned. 'Why did you follow me out of the hotel?'

'I was pretty mad, too, with Chris. He set us up, didn't he? After you left, I remembered there'd been some muggings in the area, so I left your brother to pick up the tab and followed you.'

'Serves him right,' she laughed, then added seriously, 'I'm glad you did.'

'You were doing all right till the second man jumped you. Where did you learn to defend yourself like that?'

'We were advised to take lessons before doing relief work. It could get a bit hairy, with people sometimes so desperate they'd kill for a loaf of bread, but I never had to practise self-defence out there.'

'I see.' He went quiet, brooding, his expression distant. Then he said, almost to himself, 'Chris is right on one point. It'll be damned near impossible to find a doctor at this eleventh hour, free to take off at a moment's notice, and with

20

experience in paediatrics. You'd be perfect. You've had all the necessary jabs, I suppose?'

'Of course.'

'And you've worked in Africa before, so if you were willing to come with me . . .'

An unexpected delight overrode other considerations and a smile tugged at Serena's lips.

'What I propose is that you accompany me to a safe base camp. You can stay there while I sound out the situation. I then go in alone to rescue the children, taking a guide and a camera crew. We bring them back to you and you take over their care till we get them to a hospital in Nigeria. How does that sound?'

Her hands fidgeted restlessly. A large hand reached over and covered them. 'I'm not sure,' she said.

'I promise to keep the camera crew at bay — and anyone else.' She grimaced. He'd obviously taken that 'icicle' nickname seriously. 'And I've no more desire to get involved than you have.'

He made it sound like an insult! She withdrew her hands and moved away a little. 'I still don't know.' Although it was certainly a more enticing prospect than playing gooseberry to Debbie and Simon.

'Tell me about Robbie,' Jake invited gently. 'How long ago did you lose him?'

'Four years.'

'*Four years?*' He looked stunned. 'And you're still carrying a torch for him? He must have been quite a guy!'

He was, but not in the least like Jake. 'Yes,' she agreed quietly. 'He was a fellow student; a gentle, caring man . . . '

'Was it an accident?'

'What? Oh, yes. No. Well, it was a kind of accident — a cruel accident of fate. He had a rare form of cancer, which can often now be cured. It was different then. I had to stand by and watch helplessly as his life ebbed slowly away.'

'Sorry, that sounds ghastly.'

'It was.' She had just talked about it objectively for the first time in four years, she realised. Was her heart beginning to mend at last? She looked at Jake. 'Is there someone special in your life?' she asked.

'No. Don't believe all the garbage you read in the gossip columns. I don't live like a monk — I'm not saying that — but I'm not into heavy commitment, either.'

'Perhaps you've been hurt, too,'

'Not like you,' he replied brusquely. 'How about Wadumba, then? Are you coming? Sorry to rush you, but the plane leaves in the morning.'

Serena bit her lip. She wanted to go. It was the sort of challenge she enjoyed. She wanted to go with Jake Andrews, too, she realised. He attracted her as Robbie had attracted her, but oh so differently. Robbie had been gentle and loving, while Jake exerted a powerful physical pull it might be wise to resist.

'I'll come,' she heard herself reply.

# 2

After a restless night, with doubt and insecurity keeping sleep at bay, Serena slept fitfully most of the way to Nigeria, close to the border with Wadumba. In waking moments she thought with some pleasure about Debbie's reaction when she learned who Serena's travelling companion was going to be.

'You're not going back to the Horn, are you?' she had asked, eyeing Serena's luggage in the hall.

'No. I'm going back to Africa, but to a different part, with a reporter friend of my brother's.'

'What? When was that decided?' She looked aghast as Serena filled her in on her plans. 'You can't go off with a complete stranger!'

'My brother knows him quite well — enough to vouch for him, anyway.' If only! 'Anyway, I feel like a third leg

24

round here.' Debbie had the grace to look embarrassed. 'It might be best if I move out altogether when I get back, irrespective of whether or not I get the Dorset job.'

'What about the rent?'

'Didn't you say Simon wanted to move in? Officially, I mean.'

'You don't understand — he's just lost his lecturing post. He can't afford to keep his own place, which is why he wants to move in; but I can't afford all the rent on a teacher's pay.'

'My God, Debbie, you've got a nerve. You seriously expect me to pay half the rent and keep a low profile while you two cavort about?'

'You can afford it with parents like yours,' Debbie retorted sulkily.

They had been at school together, and Debbie had always resented Serena having wealthy parents while her own had struggled to find the fees. What Debbie didn't know was that Serena hadn't accepted a penny from them since. They would have much preferred her to do something more feminine, like a cordon bleu cookery course, and meet a rich husband.

'Parents like mine,' she explained now, 'meant that since my heart was set on medicine, rather than something more frivolous, I had to go it alone, using a small legacy from my grand-mother.'

'Well, it was your choice, so you've no right to be so jealous of me and Simon,' Debbie said petulantly.

Jealous? Serena jealous of Debbie? Before she could offer up a suitable retort, the doorbell rang. She opened it to find Jake standing there, spruce, tanned and gorgeous in a pale leather jacket, cream shirt and toning trousers. She fought down a small thrill of pleasure and triumph. 'Hello, Jake,' she greeted him casually.

He grinned, his smile a slash of white against his tan. 'Good morning, Serena. All set?' His glance went past her to a puzzled Debbie.

'Oh, this is my flatmate, Debbie.'

'Hi, Debbie. I'll just take these to the car, Serena.'

Once he'd disappeared with Serena's luggage, Debbie rounded on her. 'You sly devil! You didn't say you were going off with Jake Andrews. When did you meet him?'

'About twelve hours ago.'

'I take back all I said. I'm beginning to feel a bit jealous myself. Let's not part on bad terms, Serena.'

'No, let's not,' Serena agreed with a sigh. 'But I meant what I said. A third flatmate pays a third share and does not run around half-naked.'

'I'll have a word with Simon. I do hope it works out for you. Jake's gorgeous.'

'It's work, Debbie.'

'Of course it is,' Debbie agreed with a grin, clearly unconvinced.

★   ★   ★

When the long flight ended and they stepped onto African soil, the heat hit

Serena like a wall. They were met by an official from the embassy, who looked her over doubtfully. 'Wouldn't advise taking a woman into Wadumba right now,' he said in clipped ex-army tones.

'Serena's a doctor,' Jake told him.

'She's also a woman. I've booked you into the Mirabel, and I suggest she stays there. The Jeep and all the supplies you asked for have been laid on and will be waiting for you at the landing site in Wadumba, along with your pal, Buoni.'

'Great!' said Jake with a polite smile. 'I think we both need a shower, a meal and a good night's rest. I'll get going first thing in the morning.'

Serena sat in the back of the embassy car and could hear little of what they were talking about in the front. Was that deliberate? Whatever they decided between them, she had every intention of going in with Jake and no intention of staying behind like some camp follower of old.

'Sorry about this,' Jake apologised,

closing the door on the helpful porter who had delivered their luggage to their room. George Hammond from the embassy had booked them a luxurious suite. He clearly did think Serena was there for Jake's amusement. But it wasn't a problem, as there were two bedrooms and a sitting room beside a beautiful shared bathroom. They could manage. This was far superior to any accommodation they could expect in the coming days.

'No need to apologise,' Serena said. 'This is more luxurious than I expected.'

'I didn't mean the accommodation.' Jake sighed. 'No, I'm afraid George is rather old-fashioned. He sees women as — er — companions, shall we say, and a vulnerable breed to be protected.'

'And clearly he thinks you're my protector,' she replied with studied calm. 'Let's leave the poor man to his illusions, as long as we both know where we stand.'

'Don't worry, you're safe with me.'

Once again, it sounded like an insult.

'I'm going to take a shower,' she announced.

'Serena, he has a point.' She'd almost closed the bathroom door but paused to listen. 'On the way here he told me they've lost all contact with Wadumba. The situation's worsening by the hour. I think I'll go in tonight.'

'Fine. I'll be ready.'

'No, I'm going in alone. It's far too dangerous for you.'

'Don't be absurd,' Serena scoffed. 'I didn't come all this way to kick my heels in some plush hotel, worrying about what's happening to you.'

'Would you?'

'Would I what?'

'Worry about me?'

'I meant to say 'wondering'.'

'Of course you did.' He strolled over to the drinks table and made two long, cool drinks, adding ice from the fridge.

'Thanks,' Serena said. The glass was delightfully cool, but as Jake's fingers brushed hers an unexpected heat raced around her system. She really must get a grip.

'I rather like the thought of you worrying about me,' he said quietly.

'I meant — '

'I know. You meant 'wondering'. After you with the shower.'

'If you won't take me, I could always get there under my own steam.'

'That I doubt. This is Africa.'

'Those kids need medical help and I'm here to provide it.'

'Be reasonable, Serena. It's dangerous out there. Even your numbskull brother wouldn't want to risk your neck in Wadumba. I know you can look after yourself in a one-to-one situation, but we're talking guns and armies here, not muggers.'

'And what protection do you have against them? What do you have to offer?'

'What do you mean?'

'I mean I could trade my medical skills for our safety.'

Jake glared down from his six-foot-three to her five-foot-five. 'What makes you think they'd need your medical skills?'

'What army doesn't?'

'Come on, Serena, this is getting us nowhere.'

He was gradually becoming less belligerent, and his eyes narrowed speculatively as she asked, 'What if I'm prepared to beg, borrow or steal to get there?' Sensing victory, she ventured a smile. He returned it, shaking his head resignedly.

'Tell you what — I'll take you as far as base camp. If I sense trouble there, you go straight back with the pilot. Agreed?'

'Agreed.' She gave him a winning smile. 'We both shall.'

'I didn't say that.'

For a reply, she whipped into the bathroom and closed the door with a firm clunk.

\* \* \*

The small plane skimmed low over the trees. Twenty-four hours ago, Serena had never heard of Jake Andrews. Now she was sitting beside him in a small aircraft, alone except for a surly African pilot, heading for God only knew where.

The camera crew Jake was expecting had failed to materialise in Nigeria. Instead, George Hammond received a message to say that they'd be working on another story in the region till the following day, and would then be free to join Jake at his hotel. Jake was furious.

'That's the very last time they'll be working for this television company!' he declared. 'They know time is of the essence. There's nothing for it — we'll have to go in alone.'

'Wouldn't advise it, Jake,' said George. 'You need back-up. And you can't take a woman, either.'

'Serena's a doctor.'

'We've already had this conversation.'

In the end, with Serena still determined, Jake heaved a sigh of resignation and reluctantly agreed to take her. After a last meal they took off in the small plane provided, heading for the base camp just inside Wadumba.

The light was fading fast. Keeping low, they began a rapid descent and, just when Serena thought they would surely tangle in the sturdy branches of the massive trees below, a narrow clearing came into view. The undercarriage rattled into place, ready for landing, and soon they were skimming along the bumpy, uneven ground.

They had barely stopped when the surly pilot swung out of his seat and opened the hatch. Jake leapt nimbly to the ground. The pilot handed down their luggage, then hovered impatiently while Serena jumped to the ground with a little help from Jake, who then glanced round the clearing.

'Where the hell's Buoni with the damned Jeep?' he stormed. 'Hammond assured me it was all arranged.'

As Serena scanned the endless ranks of trees for signs of human life, she felt a flutter of apprehension. The staccato sound of the hatch slamming shut brought their heads round. To their utter disbelief, the plane circled round and began its run back along the air strip.

'Hey, wait!' Jake yelled, dashing after the departing aircraft, but the only response was a grim backward glance from the pilot.

'Well, so much for Buoni's support.' Jake shrugged, attempting to make light of their predicament, but Serena wasn't fooled for a moment. 'I guess he's sleeping off his supper.'

'It's just as well we ate before we came,' she commented cheerfully. 'No five-star hotels here.'

'What did you expect?' he snapped.

'Just making small talk,' she said sweetly. 'Relax. Tell me about Buoni. Who is he, exactly?'

'Buoni is the son of a local tribal chief and a personal friend. I've known him for years. Hammond from the embassy has kept in contact with him to make sure we have everything we need, including transport. Funny . . . he's usually completely reliable.'

Night falls swiftly in the jungle and, as the light began to fade, ominous sounds of wildlife could be heard from the darkness of the trees. Serena tried not to think about the species that might be in the vicinity, many of them dangerous — in particular that wounded lioness. She was grateful for the arm Jake placed round her shoulders, and leaned towards him.

'Cold?' he asked. A chill wind had suddenly sprung up.

'A little,' she replied. And scared stiff!

'Just look at that,' he murmured into her hair, directing her gaze to the small patch of sky visible above them. Within a circle of velvety blackness framed by the treetops, a copious array of stars glinted brightly.

'They look close enough to touch,' she whispered in awe. 'They're like lanterns winking in the sky.'

'Africa never ceases to amaze,' Jake

whispered back; and as he bent closer, his lips accidentally brushed her temple. She had no desire to move away.

'Here comes Buoni,' he announced; and Serena felt his relief, as keen as hers, as an ancient Jeep sputtered through the trees to emerge in the clearing. 'That's not the healthiest-sounding of engines, I must say.'

He set off in the direction of the approaching vehicle, his arm still around Serena's shoulders. The head-lights dazzled them till the Jeep slewed round and came to a halt, lights still blazing. As it did so, half a dozen Africans poured from the vehicle, toting guns and shouting ominously.

'Christ!' Jake swore, closing his eyes in exasperation. 'Why the hell did I bring you?'

'At least you're not alone,' she retorted, sounding braver than she felt.

His breath whistled impatiently through his teeth as he released her. He strolled with studied nonchalance towards the leader — the oldest and tallest, and the one to whom the others seemed to defer — holding his hand out in friendship. 'We come in peace, so put away your guns. Do you speak English, by any chance?'

The guns remained. 'Leetle,' growled the man eventually. 'Who are you? What you want? You spies?'

'Certainly not. We're here to visit a fellow countryman — Father O'Leary.' Who was actually Irish, but why complicate matters? 'We haven't heard from him for a while and were worried he might be ill.'

'Not ill. You can go. We take you to border. She stay.'

The leader exchanged some comments with his men in their own language. They eyed her in an explicit and insulting way and, for the first time, Serena felt real fear. Surely she hadn't travelled all this way to become the spoils of war?

Jake's arm went around her once more and tightened reassuringly. He addressed the group in their own tongue, his gestures clearly possessive as he placed a large hand flat on her stomach. Whatever he said managed to wipe the grins off their faces. The group exchanged wry glances but Jake continued speaking.

'What's going on?' she hissed when he finally fell silent.

Keeping his eyes on the Africans, he said, 'I explained that you're my wife and that you're pregnant.'

'I know which bit that was,' she muttered, her skin still tingling where his hand had rested. 'What did you say after that?'

'I told them you're a doctor. I think that got to them.'

'Does that mean you're leaving me here?'

'Not on your life!'

Which might not be worth much right now, she thought.

The leader snapped an order to his men. Four of them, casting resentful backward glances, set off warily through the trees, guns at the ready. 'You get in Jeep,' he ordered Jake and Serena. He and the driver climbed up in the front while Serena and Jake took the rear seats.

'Where are you taking us?' Serena asked.

Turning round and addressing her directly for the first time, he informed her with a travesty of a smile, 'To the mission, of course.'

They negotiated the rough track that twisted through the trees, soon passing the four men on foot. Serena was glad of Jake's comforting arm and huddled against his hard, muscular chest.

'One up to us, wouldn't you say?' he murmured.

'It depends what we find at the mission,' she replied grimly.

'Let's not anticipate. I'm your husband, don't forget. I'll take care of you.'

'Except that you're not, which they'll very soon discover.'

His fingers dug into her ribs, causing her to wince. 'Do one thing to allow

40

them to think otherwise, and we're in trouble,' he growled. 'From now on we maintain the fiction that we're married. Our lives could depend on it.'

They jolted into a clearing surrounded on three sides by single-storey concrete buildings with corrugated iron roofs. Climbing plants struggled up the bleak walls, their colours and varieties indiscernible in the dim light. As the party came to a halt, they were surrounded by soldiers.

'This is the mission,' Jake told Serena.

'What happened to the base camp?'

'I dread to think. Possibly demolished, but clearly not an option as a destination.'

'You get out now!' snapped the leader.

Jake helped Serena to alight and held her protectively close as if he couldn't bear to let her go. When the leader had finished barking instructions to his men, who comprised a dozen or so — hardly a revolutionary force — Jake spoke to him. 'Has Father O'Leary retired for the night, or can we see him?'

'Why not?'

At least the priest was still alive, was Serena's cheering thought as they were led to a hut. Inside were two doors leading off a small lobby.

'He's in there.' The leader pushed open the door on the right. 'The other room is yours. I'll be back in half an hour.'

A dim oil lamp cast a glow on two narrow beds that were just thin mattresses on wooden platforms. The old man who raised himself from one of them looked at least seventy. The other bed was occupied by a small African child. He appeared to be asleep, but his slumber was broken by troubled whimpers that indicated he was in pain.

'Father O'Leary!' Serena noted the compassion on Jake's face as he helped the older man to rise and clasped him in an embrace.

'Jake Andrews? Is it really you? Or

am I hallucinating?'

'It really is!' Jake laughed. 'Large as life and twice as ugly.'

By his laughter the priest appeared to agree. 'And who have we here?' he asked, glancing beyond Jake to where Serena stood, bemused by this new compassionate Jake.

'Father, I'd like you to meet my wife, Serena.'

As they exchanged greetings, Serena felt a certain regret that it was necessary to deceive this sweet old man.

'He's a fine man, this husband of yours,' she was assured and, playing the part, she smiled up at Jake with every semblance of an adoring wife.

'As I'm discovering all the time,' she agreed, earning her a puzzled glance from Jake. 'I only hope we can help your young patients.'

'Serena's a doctor,' Jake explained. 'A paediatrician, in fact.'

'We were told you had three serious cases here,' she said.

'I'm afraid little Jimi here is the only

one left. We had a leukaemia case who might have stood a chance in a well-equipped, modern hospital, but . . . '

'I'm sorry. What happened to the boy with the broken limb?'

Serena was assuming that the one remaining patient was the bite victim, since there was no evidence of a plaster.

'His family insisted on taking him home once it began to mend, and when the 'new patients' moved in,' he ended wryly.

'Who are these new patients?'

'Wounded guerrilla fighters — a revolutionary rabble, with only Sister Monica and me to take care of them.'

'Sister Monica is here?' Jake was clearly pleased.

'She refused to leave when the rest of the nursing staff fled. Sure, she has the courage of an army. The rest slipped away into the jungle. I'm afraid some of the nuns were badly treated by the soldiers,' he added in a hushed whisper.

Serena tried not to dwell on this last piece of information which she had not been intended to hear. 'So this little chap's the bite case,' she said. Gently she lifted the thin bed covering. The boy's wounds were horrendous. There were deep gouges on his thighs, while the grooves across his back had begun to fester. She laid a hand on his forehead. His temperature was at fever level. He muttered deliriously in his sleep. Needing to act quickly, she prepared and administered a penicillin injection. The boy moaned but didn't wake. She then did what she could to make him comfortable.

'Come on, Serena, we need to inspect our accommodation,' said Jake. 'We'll see you in the morning, Father O'Leary.'

'Indeed. Sleep well. You must both be exhausted from your journey.'

The other room was similar in size to the priest's, with two narrow single beds, side by side. 'We can't ... ' Serena began.

'What do you suggest? Tell them the truth and have you fed to the mob?'

'But . . . '

'I'm equally appalled, but we'll just have to manage.'

He seemed to enjoy adding insult to injury. Before Serena could reply, there was a rap on the door. Jake opened it to find the driver standing there. 'You come now,' he said.

Serena was almost ready to drop, but the day wasn't over yet. They followed the driver to the main building: a long, low hut kitted out as a basic hospital ward. The beds, a dozen or so, were occupied by young Africans, some asleep, others awake and groaning in pain. A nun of ample dimensions was moving among them, doing what she could for them.

'Sister Monica!' called the driver.

She turned, her bright blue eyes lighting up in a well-scrubbed face at sight of Jake and Serena.

'Well, if it isn't Jake Andrews!' she called softly, coming towards them.

'What in the name of heaven are you doing here?'

'I've come to introduce my wife to my favourite nun,' he joked.

The nun's eyes twinkled over Serena. 'You're out of your mind, bringing a pretty young thing like this out here!'

'I'm here because I'm a doctor,' Serena explained. 'I came to treat some children, but it seems the patients are older.'

'Not a lot,' the nun replied drily. 'I'm delighted to meet you, my dear. I tell you now — we need to get little Jimi out of here if he's to survive.'

'I have to agree. I've given him a shot of penicillin, but he needs to be in a proper hospital. I'll take a look at these patients while I'm here, if that's all right.'

'Of course.'

The patients turned out to be victims of accidents or snake bites, while some had suffered broken limbs or merely cuts and bruises. Two had bullet wounds, but neither was life-threatening.

There was a curtained-off area at the end of the ward. 'You'll need to be careful with that one,' Sister Monica warned. 'He's Kuomi's son. If anything happens to him, it could be the end for us.'

When they slipped behind the curtain, Serena stopped short and Jake collided with her. They paused together, shocked and intrigued by the sight of Kuomi, sitting beside a youth of no more than fifteen years with a bad gunshot wound to the thigh. A tear was visible on the older man's cheek.

'This is my son,' he informed them unnecessarily. 'His name Abio, You cure, or . . . ' He drew a finger across his throat.

'I'll do my best, but ultimately it's in the lap of the gods,' Serena told him as coolly as she could. Kuomi spat to show his contempt for that philosophy.

As Abio was unconscious, Serena was

able to examine him thoroughly, with no possibility of hurting him. As she proceeded, Sister Monica explained that they had managed to remove the bullet, but because their supplies had been looted, they didn't have the antiseptics and dressings they needed for him.

Fortunately Serena had brought ample supplies and made a mental note to ensure they weren't pilfered. Maybe in the circumstances, Kuomi could prove an ally in safeguarding their supplies. She was appalled by the state of the youth. He needed far more than the simple treatment which had been available. It could already be too late.

She concentrated on her task, determined not to display her anxieties. But on the one occasion when she glanced up, she met Jake's eyes and knew she hadn't fooled him for a moment. Kuomi's son had a fifty-fifty chance, if that. Their own best chance of survival lay in getting away from here, which might well prove impossible.

Serena removed the old dressing, cleaned up the festering wound and applied a new dressing. Like Jimi, Abio received a penicillin injection to help with the infection. Having done all she could, she turned to go.

'You make better?' demanded Kuomi.

'As I said, it's not entirely up to me,' she reiterated. 'I can only do my best with the resources available, as I'm sure Father O'Leary and Sister Monica have done.'

'You cure,' Kuomi growled menacingly.

'You trot along now and get some sleep,' the nun insisted when she had finished. 'You both look fit to drop.'

'Yes, come on, darling,' Jake agreed evenly. 'Time to turn in. I hope we'll be accorded some privacy.' He directed these last words to the chief, who was standing nearby, in view of the way he had burst into the priest's room unannounced.

'You will,' came the grudging reply.

Two soldiers escorted them across the compound, leaving them at the door of their hut. They entered, closed the door, and were then alone.

# 3

'So what now?' Serena asked warily.

'Two beds but only one blanket and one mosquito net — we'll have to manage. And no arguments. As Sister Monica surmised, I, for one, am fit to drop. Your virtue is safe with me tonight.'

But what about the next night, and the next? Serena wondered as he pushed open an inner door to reveal a primitive bathroom.

'You go first,' he said.

She returned feeling quite self-conscious in her simple cotton nightshirt and slid into one of the beds, while Jake went through to wash. Despite her first instinct to feign sleep, she couldn't resist watching with half-closed eyelids as he returned. He was wearing boxer shorts and she enjoyed watching his neat, precise movements as he climbed into the other bed and adjusted the mosquito net. At that point she turned her back to him, taking care not to dislodge the shared blanket.

'Serena?' he whispered, after a while.

She toyed with the idea of feigning sleep but knew he wouldn't be fooled. 'What is it?' she muttered.

'Turn round. We need to talk.' She hesitated. 'Come on, Serena. Turn round. I can't talk to the back of your head.'

Reluctantly she complied. He had left the light on beside his bed and it came as a shock to find herself face to face with him at such close quarters. His eyes, fringed by long black lashes, were darkest jade; his hair like jet against the stark white linen of the pillow, its pristine condition doubtless due to Sister Monica's efforts.

'How bad is Abio?' he asked quietly.

'Very. He's got blood poisoning from wounds and they've gone septic. If we can cure that he'll probably pull through. I'm also concerned about little Jimi. He needs urgent hospital treatment. They both do, but I guess Kuomi wouldn't take kindly to having his son carted off.'

'From what I've seen this is a very minor rebellion. I chatted with some of the other patients and it seems their grievances don't amount to much. Our arrogant leader saw a chance to grab himself some glory and jumped on the bandwagon, but it's gone wrong. Storming government offices did little damage except to themselves. Now Kuomi's men, in fact little more than teenagers, are sick, wounded and frightened — they know they could face jail or worse if they're caught. You can be sure the authorities are looking for them. Father O'Leary's radio message was cut off because Kuomi smashed the radio. We need to keep Kuomi's son alive till government troops get here, or till we get Jimi out. We came to help children, after all, and he's the only child left.' He smiled suddenly. 'You did very well, by the way, Mrs Andrews — my serene, calm-in-a-crisis Serena.'

'You didn't do so badly yourself, Mr Andrews.'

He grinned. 'As I've already said, I think on my feet.'

'And come up with the most outlandish solutions.'

'I thought it rather good, myself,' he said smugly. 'I can't think of anyone I'd rather have as the temporary Mrs Andrews.'

That said it all — the *temporary* Mrs Andrews. Which, in such an intimate situation, it could be all too easy to forget. 'As you say — *very* temporary.'

He was so close, so very close. 'We may become addicted to each other.'

Didn't she just know it? For him, the addiction would cloy all too soon, with his determination to avoid commitment. While for her . . . ?

He lifted a hand and brushed a strand of blond hair away from her face. At the light touch of his fingers she half closed her eyes, shivering despite the

55

heat coming off his body. He raised himself on one elbow and devoured her with his gaze. Then he leaned over and kissed her. It was brief, but deeply pleasurable, and Serena knew for certain that her love for Robbie had been gently relegated to the past.

'You're very beautiful,' he said conversationally before turning his back and switching off the light.

Serena felt as though she had just fallen asleep when a tap on the door woke her.

'Come in!' came Jake's voice, startling her awake.

Serena sat up swiftly, recalling the events of the previous day and the unfulfilled yearnings of the night. Jake's bed was empty.

Jake wandered in from the bathroom at the same time as Sister Monica entered, drying his smoothly shaved chin in an endearingly domestic gesture.

'Good morning to you both,' she greeted them in her cheerful Irish voice.

'I hope you're comfortable here. This accommodation is intended for the families of nuns when they visit. I've brought you some breakfast.'

'Wonderful,' said Serena, 'and yes, we're very comfortable here, thanks.' Speak for yourself, she thought; she had lain awake for hours. 'You shouldn't be waiting on us, though.'

Jake strolled over and raised the mosquito net. 'Thank you,' said Serena, forcing herself to smile at her 'husband'. 'Is that real coffee?'

'Yes, we've not run out of everything yet. As to waiting on you, I'm off to my bed now. Father O'Leary will be taking over. That's how we've managed since the others disappeared. He does the days, I do the nights. Of course there's more to do in the day, so I'm sure he'll be keeping you both busy.'

'How's Jimi?' asked Serena.

'I'm delighted to say he's no worse at the least, and possibly a mite or two better.'

The nun smiled her twinkling smile

and Serena responded in kind, then frowned as she remembered.

'And Abio?'

'He's drifted into a coma, I'm afraid,' came the quiet reply. 'We could be in a bit of trouble there,' she added. It was a massive understatement.

'I have an idea,' Jake announced, appearing to change the subject. 'Is there any possibility of mending the radio?'

'For someone who knew what he was doing, perhaps,' replied Sister Monica.

'You don't imagine Kuomi would let you near it for one second, do you?' Serena began scornfully. 'Why . . . ' Suddenly aware of Sister Monica's expression, she came to a stumbling halt. Jake lowered himself to the bed beside her, one bare arm encircling her shoulders, green eyes flashing a warning.

'Darling, I know you're jumpy, but I do have a plan of sorts.'

'Sorry, darling,' she returned contritely, earning a look of admiration from Jake and one of approval from the nun. 'I didn't mean to snap.'

She might have known he would take advantage of her contrition, massaging her shoulders and thereby increasing the tension he supposedly intended to soothe. To the onlooker it may have appeared a loving gesture intended to calm, but it was having quite the opposite effect on Serena's stretched nerves.

'I know.' He pressed a kiss to her temple and she had to glance away from the wicked humour in his eyes. He was amusing himself at her expense! 'What I thought was that first we must persuade Kuomi that the radio is essential for *him*, but we use it ourselves to get a message out.'

'An interesting idea,' Serena said, 'but how will we persuade the man?'

'Well, Abio is, as you are aware, in a coma. Sometimes patients are helped back to consciousness by familiar sounds — people talking and laughing, or playing the kind of music the patient would enjoy. Isn't that a fact?'

'It's happened in a few cases.'

'It's a shame we're out of CDs,' laughed Sister Monica, 'but the next best thing would be — '

'The radio,' finished Serena.

'Precisely!'

'But once it's fixed, Kuomi will certainly confiscate it,' Serena said.

Jake smiled at her. 'So he mustn't know until our messages have been sent — always assuming I can fix it.'

'Good luck, anyway,' Sister Monica said. 'I'm off to my bed now. I have a little apartment at the end of the hospital block. You'll find me there if you need me.' She closed the door behind her.

'I guess I owe you an apology for last night,' Jake said to Serena when they were alone.

'Apology?'

'I had no right to kiss you. I promised you no unwelcome advances, but I seldom find myself in such a situation and having to behave like a monk. So I'm sorry.'

'Let's forget it.'

'Done. I worry about Sister Monica and Father O'Leary. I don't know how they keep going. They've been running the place alone, one by day, the other by night.'

'I know. They must be exhausted. They're not young.' She tried to shake off the hand still clamped to her shoulder. 'You can stop the adoring husband act now, Jake.'

'You do realise you came close to giving the game away just now?' he whispered harshly.

She coloured. 'I thought I retrieved the situation rather well,' she declared defiantly. 'Now will you kindly remove your hand!'

'You look extremely kissable this morning, Mrs Andrews,' he murmured, his eyes sparkling with devilment.

'Stop it, Jake.'

Instead his lips captured hers and she responded despite herself. She pulled away, furious with herself for acting and feeling like that living Barbie doll. He regarded her with an inscrutable expression then calmly removed his signet ring. 'You'd better wear this,' he said, thrusting it onto her ring finger. Then he turned and disappeared back into the bathroom.

Serena studied the ring. Exquisitely monogrammed, it felt heavy on her slender finger. She wondered who had given it to him. Till now it had been on his little finger, and she experienced an unexpected tenderness as she ran her thumb over its surface.

What on earth was happening to her? She had never reacted to a man as she had to Jake — not even Robbie. It must be due to the unusual circumstances they were in. Jake wasn't her type, she told herself. He was too handsome, too self-assured, too undeniably male. He had also expressed a determination to remain free and unencumbered.

'I'll accompany you to the hospital when you're ready,' he informed her, coming out of the bathroom. 'Can't have you wandering about on your own. In the meantime, I'll be with Father O'Leary.'

'Thanks,' she mumbled, unable to meet his eyes.

He had strung a line across the bathroom, so before joining him she hung her dainty underwear and yesterday's shirt beside his. How domestic, she thought, but how embarrassing — although probably not for him. He was doubtless all too familiar with ladies' underwear. The thought caused a pang of some unfamiliar emotion.

In the hospital, Serena greeted the priest before examining Jimi. This morning he was lying with his eyes open. She smiled with delight as she laid a cool hand on his forehead, noting that his temperature felt quite normal. 'Hello, Jimi. How are you?' The little boy smiled back — an encouraging sign — and said something in his own tongue.

'He wants to know if he's in heaven. He thinks you look like an angel,' Father O'Leary translated.

'You'd better assure him I'm flesh and blood, just like him.' She kept her eyes on Jimi as she spoke. A telling grunt came from Jake, close beside her, for her ears alone. She wanted to turn and glare at him but thought better of it. 'Tell him I'm here to make him better.' She turned and smiled sweetly at her supposed husband. He returned the smile, mocking amusement in the green depths of his eyes.

'And to sweeten my existence, of course,' he offered maddeningly.

'Of course,' she agreed, placing a hand on his muscled forearm and giving him a sly pinch.

He stifled an exclamation but his eyes threatened retribution.

'Has Jimi had his first dose of medicine today?' Serena asked, returning to practicalities.

'Sure,' Father O'Leary replied, 'and he took it like a man.'

'I should hope so — it tastes of strawberries. I'll change his dressings now. Tell him I'll do my very best not to hurt him.'

He took the treatment like a man, too, she had to admit later, knowing it must have been painful for the little boy. 'How did it happen?' she asked the priest as she worked.

'He was playing on the edge of his village by himself when the lioness pounced.'

'So how did he manage to escape?' asked Jake, fascinated by Serena's skilled and gentle touch.

'His father and uncle heard his screams and went to his assistance. Eventually his uncle was able to free him, but unfortunately his father died in the attempt.'

'The poor boy,' Serena murmured. Her tender heart went out to him — what a horrible experience.

'Shall we be looking at the other patients now?' asked Father O'Leary.

'Certainly,' Serena agreed, fighting down the worry that the chief's son, Abio, could be worse today.

She took in the layout of the mission in the bright daylight. Neat buildings were ranged along three sides of the compound, their starkness alleviated by the brilliant red and purple of the bougainvillaea that rioted over the walls. Tubs of scarlet and pink geraniums added another splash of colour.

The ward round consisted of changing dressings and administering medicines. Jake proved a surprisingly helpful assistant. If he felt squeamish, he disguised it well. The priest remained on hand to explain things to the patients where necessary. He also added to Serena's limited supply of dressings by cutting up some old sheets, well boiled, into strips. Finally, they reached the curtain drawn around the bed at the end of the ward.

Serena was surprised that Kuomi hadn't appeared earlier, to demand priority attention for his son. However, when they drew back the curtain, they found not Kuomi but a native woman, clutching Abio's hand and crying copiously — Abio's mother, they assumed.

'Would you explain to her why I'm here?' Serena asked Father O'Leary. 'Tell her that tears are useless. She'd do better to sing and talk to him. I'll give him another shot of antibiotics and change his dressings.'

'Mara,' the priest called gently and proceeded to talk to her in her own tongue.

Serena had just completed his dressings when Kuomi appeared. There was little doubt about the abuse Mara was shouting at her husband.

'Ahem!' Jake cleared his throat. 'Father O'Leary, could you ask about the radio and explain our plan — to help their son?' he clarified. 'You're sure there's no other source of music?'

'None.'

The boy's mother, Mara, caught on first. 'Beatles! Beatles!' she cried, her face momentarily lighting up.

'Can't promise the Beatles,' Jake said. 'It's more likely to be Eminem or the like. I can't actually promise anything; but if he agrees, I'll do my best to fix the radio.'

Kuomi's mistrust and suspicions were overcome by Mara's ceaseless haranguing, so Jake soon had the chief's authority to try to repair the radio. 'Better be success,' he growled, with a shifty look at his wife. 'You tell me when mended. I keep radio when working. Only I have it.' Which was precisely the attitude they'd expected.

When they emerged from the hospital block, the heat was stifling. In the yard a group of Kuomi's men were taking turns working the pump that supplied water from the bore hole and filling the reserve tank with fresh supplies. That would have been one of the nuns' tasks, Serena surmised, and she wondered if they would ever return.

Jake and the priest nodded a greeting to the group. Serena did not. She wasn't at all well-disposed to men who would have carelessly used her the night before, given the chance. She gave them a brief glance, though, surprising one of them doing an exaggerated impression of a feminine wiggle. Looking up, she caught Jake sucking in his cheeks in an attempt not to laugh. There was even a glint of humour in the priest's eyes.

'I do not wiggle,' she said primly through tight lips.

'Oh but you do, my love,' he informed her, adding, 'I'm happy to say.'

It was too much — the false endearments and enforced proximity to this chauvinistic male. She stormed over to the hapless young soldiers. She could mime, too!

'You and you,' she snapped, jabbing a finger towards her chosen victims. She pointed at the hospital block and picked up an imaginary broom, leaving them in no doubt as to what was expected of them. 'Get along now.'

Nor had she finished. She pointed at a bucket and mimed floor-washing. 'You and you!'

The chosen pair ambled off in the

wake of the other two, half-grumbling, half-chuckling. They now knew who the blond lady was and also that their mates, brothers and cousins could owe their lives to her skills.

'Right then,' she said, still in organising mode. 'I'll go and help Father O'Leary prepare lunch and amuse Jimi while you go and play with your radio — darling,' she tacked on for good measure.

There was no shortage of hands to prepare vegetables, nor to wring the necks of two of the precious flock of chickens and prepare them for the pot — not something Serena was keen to do. The resultant stew, flavoured with herbs, spices and chillies, was delicious.

'You've been a great help, my dear,' said the priest when the meal was ready. 'You'd better go and fetch that husband of yours — he must be starving.'

It sounded so normal — 'that husband of yours'. Serena almost wished they weren't deceiving the old priest. But if they weren't . . . ?

Jake was working in the shade of an awning rigged up outside the office. He didn't hear Serena approach, and she was able to pause and watch him for a while. Parts of the shattered radio were lined up on the table in front of him; the muscles of his back and shoulders rippled under his cotton T-shirt. His dark head was bent, his shadowed eyes rapt in concentration. A lock of hair had fallen onto his brow. His long, elegant fingers were deftly handling fine pieces of wire and minute radio components. Serena recalled how it felt to be held in those arms and soothed by those fingers.

Her breath caught, a barely audible sound alerting Jake to her presence. His head came up sharply. 'What is it? he demanded brusquely as if he resented her intrusion into his thoughts.

'Lunch — darling,' she tacked on sweetly. 'Father O'Leary thought you deserved to eat.'

He stood up, pushing the chair back

and strolling towards her. Inches away, his hands came up to rest either side of her waist, his head swooping to capture her lips with his own.

It was a mere brushing of his lips across hers, hardly justifying the heat that flooded through her system, the pulse throbbing inside her, the sudden difficulty in breathing. She prided herself on being cool and in control — what on earth was happening to her? The heat must be affecting her brain. Funny, it hadn't happened on her last trip to Africa.

'And what does my beautiful wife think?' he enquired softly, drawing her against him.

The warmth coming off him teased her nostrils. This close, she could see a fine sheen of moisture on his tanned skin and a dark flush across his cheekbones. Lifting her eyes a little higher, she recognised stark desire in the wonderful green eyes, and an answering need uncoiled within her. Beautiful, he had called her . . .

'I suppose we can't let you starve,' she commented lightly, controlling the tremor in her voice. 'How's the repair coming along?'

He leaned to whisper in her ear, in the attitude of a loving husband. 'I can probably do it by tomorrow. I'll tell Kuomi it'll most likely take three days. Okay?'

'There's no one to see, so you can stop nibbling my earlobe.'

'I like nibbling your earlobe.' He grinned, sliding an arm about her waist and falling into step beside her.

# 4

While Father O'Leary, assisted by the able-bodied, looked after the injured, Serena spent time with Jimi. They were able to communicate pretty well without an interpreter. Serena adored children, which was why she had chosen paediatrics; and Jimi, after all, was a bright, rewarding child, besides being a brave one. She discovered some board games on the priest's shelves, and she and Jimi were enjoying a game of Snakes & Ladders when Jake walked in, followed by Sister Monica.

'Sister Monica has made some excellent lemonade,' said Jake. 'We thought you might like some.' He rested a hand on Serena's warm brow.

'Fantastic!' She helped herself to two glasses from the nun's tray, handing one to Jimi. 'Here you are, Jimi — lemonade.'

'Lemonade,' he repeated, flashing white teeth.

'Are you sure you've had enough sleep?' she asked Sister Monica with concern.

'Oh, I need very little sleep. Will you just look at him — he's a different child. It's incredible what modern medicine will do, and a little loving care.' She beamed a fond smile at Serena. 'You'll make a wonderful mother, my dear. Don't you agree, Jake?'

He stared at Serena through narrowed eyes, as if seeing a new facet of her for the first time. 'I certainly do. We'd like at least four.'

'Excellent! Excellent!' Sister Monica bustled out, none the wiser.

'You swine! How could you?'

'Look, he may not understand our language,' Jake remonstrated, indicating a puzzled-looking Jimi, 'but children glean a lot from atmosphere. Don't upset him, all right?'

She turned her back on him but

offered a bright smile to Jimi. 'Shall we continue our game?' she asked with a gesture.

Jake had stomped off before she'd had the time to ask about progress with the radio. Perhaps it was better for her not to know. She wasn't very good at hiding her feelings. She fervently hoped Jake hadn't guessed them from her expression — feelings about him that she could barely define herself.

Father O'Leary looked after Jimi while Serena joined Sister Monica in the hospital wing. Abio's mother was with her son, Serena was pleased to see, talking to him and softly singing tunes that sounded like lullabies.

Night fell swiftly as usual, and it was time to settle the patients. 'You get along, my dear,' said Sister Monica, unaware that Serena was dreading being alone with Jake, 'or Jake will never forgive us. You've hardly seen each other all day long.'

'If you're sure there's nothing more I can do?'

'Get along with you.' She spoke to two young Africans hovering in the doorway. 'These young men will see you across the yard. You're a heroine to them now, with your magic penicillin. Some of their friends are getting better and they'll be pleased to do something for you in return.'

'Thank you, Sister Monica. Good night.'

Halfway across the yard, Serena caught sight of Jake leaning on the door jamb of their hut, watching their approach. His very presence made her feel protected and cared for, crazy as that may be. She pinned a wifely smile to her face. 'Sister Monica detailed a bodyguard for me,' she explained.

Jake thanked her escorts in their own tongue and they sauntered off. Now they were alone, with another night to face, in that shared room. How on earth could Serena cope when the very sight of Jake set her heart pounding in her ribcage like a wild thing? Her palms felt hot and her fingertips were tingling with a desire to reach out and touch him. He looked as though he had just showered; his hair was still damp, his shirt pristine. Her own clothes, in comparison, felt hot and sticky. She would like to strip off and soak in a bath and then stand for hours under a cool shower. Some chance, with water so scarce.

'There's some cold beer — a treat from Father O'Leary, if you fancy one,' said Jake, following her in and closing the door.

'How kind of him,' she replied somewhat stiltedly, nervous now they were alone. 'I need to shower and change first, though.'

'Help yourself.'

There was little point lingering in the primitive bathroom and she soon emerged, wearing her respectable cotton nightshirt, freshly washed that morning, and wondering why Jake had bothered to dress. She came to a standstill at the sight of him sprawled on his bed, a can of beer in one hand, the other thrown back against the pillows.

'It's all right, I don't bite. Come and join me,' he invited casually.

'I'm okay here.' She had perched on the upright chair.

'For heaven's sake, come here and relax. You've been on your feet all day.'

'I prefer to sit here.'

He moved like a large, graceful panther. Setting down his can, he reached across the gap and, his fingers encircling her narrow wrist, jerked her to the bed beside him. They rolled over and she ended half-pinned to the bed by the weight of his body. Blue eyes nervously met green.

'You're not scared, are you?' he taunted softly.

Well yes, she was terrified, and not just of him! She was scared to death by the way she felt. Serena liked to feel in control of her life. Jake Andrews threw her off balance all too easily, though wild horses wouldn't drag such an admission from her.

'Not in the least,' she retorted.

'Right, well, the sooner you accept that I don't intend to jump you at every opportunity, the better. You prefer me not to touch you, right?'

'R-right,' she agreed, bewildered, for what was he doing right now?

It wasn't right, either. She ached for him to hold her close to his long, lean body and kiss her senseless. She wanted those elegant hands to caress her till she was on fire for him. He released her and sat up.

'I've got the message, Serena. Here, enjoy your beer.'

She struggled to a sitting position and accepted the cold drink. 'How's the radio coming along?'

'It's nearly done. I've just got to finish putting it together.' He drained his can and stood up. 'I intend to carry on with it while you get some kip.'

'But . . . '

'Yes?'

'Nothing. I thought you'd be as tired

as I am, that's all,' she muttered uneasily.

'Don't start feeling sorry for me, Serena. You'll spoil the cool image. Bolt the door after me. I'll knock three times when I want to come back in.'

She fixed the mosquito net and settled down, but sleep eluded her for hours. Perversely, with Jake gone, she could think only of the previous night and the comfort of his warm, vital presence in the room. What on earth was happening to her? Was she, at last, falling in love again?

The jungle settled about the mission like a blanket. Punctuating the incessant susurration of the cicadas came the occasional screech of a monkey or the shriek of some night bird. She was just drifting off to sleep when she heard a sound that made her blood run cold — a lion roaring in the night-dark jungle, or more likely a lioness. The jungle petered out not far away, giving way to plains, the vast savannah of central Africa where lions and other beasts roamed.

Only a lion too desperate to hunt its usual prey would stray near human habitation. Was this the lioness that had injured little Jimi and killed his father? Was the little boy asleep or was he, too, listening to the sound, with a terror born of experience? And where was Jake? She wished he was here. Would he be safe from that hungry animal? What would she do if anything happened to him? Oh God, it was happening — she was falling in love, with Jake.

She couldn't be, insisted the rational part of her mind. It had to be an illusion, brought on by the extraordinary circumstances that had thrown them together. Once back on familiar ground, she would forget the fascination the man held for her. Yes, once back home, she would put Jake Andrews right out of her system with the greatest of ease.

Wouldn't she?

At last she fell asleep, but her slumber was punctuated by troubled dreams. She dreamt of Jake wandering through the jungle in the cold, dark night, pursued by a limping, silent beast, its eyes yellow lanterns in the darkness.

At four o'clock in the morning there were three taps on the door. She didn't respond immediately. The knocking was incorporated into her ongoing nightmare, becoming twigs snapping underfoot, alerting the lioness to Jake's presence.

'Jake!' she yelled, sitting up.

'Serena? Are you all right? Who's in there? Serena, open this door at once!'

Reality flooded back, and an embarrassed Serena untangled herself from the mosquito net and sped across to the door.

'What's going on?' Jake demanded irritably, scowling in the dim light of the oil lamp Serena had left burning low, too scared to be entirely in the dark.

'I-I was having a dream,' she admitted, taking in the weariness etched in every line of his face and body.

'You were calling my name,' he accused.

'Yes, I-I . . . ' She recounted her nightmare, too tired to dissemble.

'Would it have bothered you that much if I'd been eaten by a lion?' He brushed some strands of hair from her face with gentle fingers and she met the stillness of his expression with wary eyes.

'I — er — well, as you pointed out, this is not the safest place for a woman alone,' she managed at last. His mouth curved in mock amusement. 'Dare I ask how the radio's coming along?'

'I've fixed it.'

'You have?'

Without thinking, she threw her arms round his neck. His arms enclosed her at once, gathering her close, and she realised he wasn't all that tired. She tried to extricate herself but his embrace tightened.

'Mm, this is nice to come home to,'

he murmured teasingly. 'As I was saying, I'd got the thing fixed and was about to try and send a message, when who should come snooping by but Kuomi himself.'

'So he knows?'

Jake had loosened his hold, but why struggle free when they were discussing something of such vital importance? Serena rested against his lean body, her arms still around his neck, her fingers curling idly into the dark hair at his nape.

'He doesn't, actually. As luck would have it, I was listening out for him. I heard his sneaky approach and quickly wrenched a couple of wires free. It won't be difficult to replace them, but I told Kuomi it would take a day or two to finish the job.'

'Whereas in reality?'

'Whereas tomorrow, with a bit of luck, I'll be able to get a message to the proper authorities. Could you create a diversion while I do that?'

'Such as?'

'I don't give a damn! Turn cartwheels across the compound in your knickers for all I care!'

'There's no need to be crude,' she replied tersely, extricating herself.

'Sorry, I didn't mean to offend, but this is important. See what you can come up with — preferably something noisy, okay?'

'Okay.'

'Now back to bed with you. I'm going to take a shower.'

It was too early to consider getting up, and Sister Monica would think it strange if she abandoned her 'husband', so she curled up in bed. When Jake climbed into his, she felt safe and protected and was soon fast asleep.

She woke as dawn was sending its first golden fingers of light through cracks in the shutters. Jake would probably sleep for hours. He must be so tired. She turned to look at him. Black lashes lay against high, well-defined cheekbones. His wide, generous mouth, softer in sleep, made him appear younger. That wayward lock of hair had flopped endearingly onto his brow, adding a curious vulnerability. She reached over and gently stroked it back.

His eyes snapped open. She felt as though she'd been caught with her fingers in the cookie jar. A sun-bronzed hand locked round her wrist. His eyes glinted with humour, and fury bubbled up inside her. He'd probably been awake all the time.

'Good morning, Mrs Andrews,' he murmured, his voice a soft growl. He turned her hand in his and planted a kiss on her palm.

'Jake, stop it. I only turned so that we could talk without eavesdroppers over-hearing,' she improvised helplessly.

'That's what I thought,' he replied, humouring her but not releasing her hand.

'Jake, please.'

He inspected her hand, seemingly fascinated by its shape, and pressed a kiss to each fingertip. 'So talk, or come over here and put me out of my misery.'

Words dried in her throat. Visions of finding solace in his embrace flickered through her mind. She wanted nothing more; but for her, love had to figure in the equation. He merely wanted to find physical release, and in these restrictive circumstances with her, as the only woman around . . .

'I — I . . . ' She was saved from further discussion by a sharp rap on the door.

Jake released her hand and called, 'Just a moment.' He pulled on some clothes before admitting Sister Monica. As he explained to the nun about the strategy he intended to use to send his message, Serena's attention was only half-engaged. The other half was still on the yearnings he had awoken in her for something she could never have. He wanted her, but that was all. He'd made it clear that he wasn't into commitment, whereas Serena's heart was already committed. She had loved Robbie and believed it to be the real, forever type of love, but it paled before this powerful feeling she had for Jake. It would be difficult, but there was no way she could have an affair without love and commitment simply because circumstances had thrown them together. An attractive, virile man like Jake Andrews would never be short of female company, and Serena didn't intend to satisfy his temporary needs. She wanted far more than Jake was prepared to give to a relationship — which was a pity; for, as Serena now realised without a shadow of doubt, she had fallen in love with him.

'Well, I'm sure Serena and I will think of something,' Sister Monica was saying. 'I'm off to my bed now, but I'll be up again at lunchtime. As I've already mentioned, at my age I have little need of sleep.'

Jake picked up the tray brought by the nun and carried it over to Serena.

'I wonder how old Sister Monica is,' Serena mused, as she poured coffee for them both.

'Do you?' he queried drily, not in the

least fooled by her change of subject. 'Then wonder no more — she's eighty-three.'

'What?' Serena almost spilled her coffee. 'I'd have put her in her mid-sixties.'

'Amazing, isn't she?' He bit into a crusty roll. 'She and Father O'Leary are from the same village. I've heard they were childhood sweethearts. They fell out and he took holy orders. She was devastated but eventually became engaged to his brother. That wasn't meant to be, though. He died in a tragic accident on the family farm, and she followed Father O'Leary into the church. They've been together, as friends, for decades.'

'How sweet, but how sad.'

'They're not at all sad, though, are they? But it's not the life for everyone. I wonder where we'll be when we're in our eighties.'

'I can't see you as a priest,' she retorted acidly.

'Oddly enough, I can't see you as a

nun! You've got that touch-me-not expression down to a T, but we both know that's a sham, don't we?'

'Give it a rest, Jake.' She slid out of bed. 'I have work to do.'

'You and I have unfinished business, Mrs Andrews. Sooner or later we're going to finish it, make no mistake.'

His words shivered about her with soft menace, but Serena had to admit the effect was as exciting as it was alarming. As she washed and dressed for another scorching day, she resolved to be doubly on guard against Jake but also against her reactions to him.

How could she have allowed herself to fall for him? She thought of Robbie and the sweet love they had shared — a tender love that had grown out of friendship and shared interests, but without that heady spark of desire she felt for Jake. So had she really been in love with Robbie? She had certainly thought so at the time. So was it merely lust she felt for Jake?

No, it was more than that. She really

cared about him. He was strong and amusing, but also the most attractive man she had ever met. She had known him only a few days, yet the prospect of a future without him seemed endlessly bleak and lonely.

How different things had been with Robbie. They had known each other for over a year when they realised they had feelings for each other. They had still been happy to go out with the crowd as often as not. Six months later, just after they became engaged, he had become ill and Serena had had to watch him slowly die.

She tried to picture Robbie's face, but it was hazy. The face imprinted on her mind was lean and handsome, with a lock of black hair flopping onto his brow and eyes that varied between green and turquoise, according to mood.

So could this be love, after such a short acquaintance? she asked herself. She had known Robbie for ages; their feelings had crept up on them slowly.

There had been a gentle caring between them, but none of the aching need that sprang into being at a touch or even a look from Jake. It was madness, sheer tropical madness — yet Serena knew she would miss him as she had never missed anyone else when they returned to England's cool grey skies.

*   *   *

'Jimi keeps asking when he can go home,' Father O'Leary informed her later that evening.

'Does he indeed?' She checked Jimi's temperature and pulse. They were normal. The antibiotics were working their miracle, and the fever ebbed as the poisons were driven out. The wounds had not yet healed, of course, and there would be permanent scars; but even they were beginning to heal.

'This is no place for a sick child, to my way of thinking,' said the old priest. 'Given the right medicine, he'd be better off with his family till they can get him to a proper hospital.'

'Why wasn't he taken straight away?'

'He needed emergency treatment and we were closer. A long journey might have killed him. Then the soldiers arrived and we became virtual hostages.'

Serena thought about the radio that would soon be mended. 'I think you're right, but if the opportunity arises he should still be taken to a hospital. I'll have a word with Jake.'

They did the ward round together, Serena and the priest. When they reached Abio's bed at the end of the ward, they were surprised to find his mother seated beside him and smiling. She chatted away happily to Father O'Leary, who translated for Serena.

'Apparently while she was singing during the night he suddenly gripped her fingers,' he said.

'That's excellent news!' Serena exclaimed, though she thought it could defeat their plan if the boy came round too soon.

'I know what you're thinking. I've spoken to Jake,' he said, keeping the tone conversational.

Was that why they wanted Jimi to go home — to spare him further trauma if the regular army were to storm the camp?

True to her word, Sister Monica was with them by lunchtime. 'I've been thinking about what Jake was saying this morning,' she said to Serena in her enchanting Irish accent as they loaded the lunch trolley. 'How well do you know Beatles songs?'

'I could sing along with a ballad or two,' she replied with a laugh.

'I was thinking more of the rock numbers.'

'The noisy ones?'

'The young nuns always enjoyed listening to them, bless them, and I reckon our sick young Abio might appreciate a sing-song with his friends. What do you think?'

'I think it's a wonderful idea,' Serena said, smiling.

'You'd better ask that husband of yours when the best time would be.'

'I'll do that.'

She would talk about Jimi, too.

# 5

Serena had her chance over lunch. She and Jake ate alone, which she figured wouldn't be considered strange. They were, after all, a young married couple.

'So you're pre-empting the radio idea,' was Jake's reaction. 'Well, why not?'

'It was Sister Monica's idea.'

'No, that's fine. It could possibly bring Abio round and also mask the sound of any message I manage to send. Put the idea about right away, and when we get Kuomi here to listen to the kids singing, as I'm sure he'd want to be, I'll quickly fix the radio and send a message.'

'I'll do that. But, Jake . . . '

'What is it?'

'What will happen to Kuomi and his band of rebels when the government troops arrive?'

'They'll probably be told to go home and stop being ridiculous. They're only kids, after all. Kuomi might be locked up as an example. They've not done a lot of harm, except to themselves. Now, you know what to do?' She nodded. 'Good. Once I hear singing — loud, preferably — I'll endeavour to get a message through.'

'Oh, there's something else, Jake. Father O'Leary thinks Jimi should be with his family, and I'm inclined to agree. He's had enough trauma for one little boy.'

'Ye-es, I think you're both right.'

'Can we get him home safely?'

'It probably can't happen till the government troops have dealt with the rebels.'

'Well, the sooner, the better.'

With no more to be said, Serena left him to his repairs. By late afternoon she had put the word around about the planned sing-song. As she was finishing her ward round, Kuomi appeared. 'Your men are mostly on the mend,' she told him brightly. 'They'll be able to leave here soon.'

'Not go yet,' he growled.

'We've thought of something that might bring Abio out of his coma, which we can do without waiting for the radio,' she told him. He listened as she explained, his naturally surly expression lifting a little. In fact, he almost smiled.

'You try now,' he ordered.

They'd reached the curtained-off area, where Mara sat, silent and anxious. 'Whenever you can spare the time,' Serena said evenly. 'You'll want to be there, of course.'

'Of course,' Kuomi agreed reluctantly, casting Mara a subdued glance, clearly in awe of the lady and her temper.

He turned to address the other patients, shouting instructions. Bemused, they gathered round. Serena tentatively launched them on the first song. She needn't have worried, as they were soon singing with enthusiasm and even suggesting numbers to sing. They had just embarked on their fourth song when Mara cried out, her strong teeth gleaming as she smiled. Those who could walk crowded closer, falling silent.

'He grip my hand!' cried a delighted Mara.

'We'd best carry on, then,' said Sister Monica.

'Did we wake you?' Serena asked ruefully.

'No, but I heard something that sounded like the crackling of a radio just now,' she explained quietly.

'Terrific!' Serena enthused.

'It wouldn't do for anyone else to hear.'

'You're right. Let's sing something noisier.'

'Sure, this lot's enough to wake the dead, but look at the boy's eyelids. Are they not flickering?'

They were, no doubt about it, nor about his mother's joy. Sister Monica launched into another song during a brief silence.

They were into the third verse when, with the sixth sense she had developed where Jake was concerned, Serena knew he was standing right behind her. She turned, her eyes locking with his before dropping to the child in his arms, young Jimi.

'He didn't want to miss all the fun,' said Jake.

She lifted an eyebrow in silent query. He nodded briefly and made a shushing expression, then added his rich baritone to the singing. 'You can stop any time you like,' he whispered as the song ended.

'It's working?' Serena whispered back.

'It is. I suggest you send this lot about their business. We have things to do.'

She stood beside Mara and clapped her hands, sending the singers on their way while Jake spoke to Kuomi in his own tongue. Serena could only guess what was said from their expressions, but Jake seemed to be persuading Mara to his way of thinking. Good move! Mara began to gesticulate and argue for Jake.

'What was all that about?' Serena asked as they walked away, Jake still holding Jimi.

'Kuomi's going to let this little chap go home, accompanied by Sister Monica and Father O'Leary.'

'Wonderful! He's letting them both go?'

'Yes — one to drive, the other to hold Jimi. Unfortunately, he refused to allow you to go with them, too.'

'What? You mean you asked him? You don't think I'd leave you here alone!' she stormed, not caring what she gave away in her fury.

He sighed impatiently. 'You don't have that choice! I guess we're now the hostages.'

She felt a stab of fear, but at least they'd be together.

'Why the hell did I bring you?'

'I insisted,' she reminded him.

'So you did, dammit!'

Some time later, she watched with a heavy heart as the old Jeep rumbled away, carrying Jimi; the old priest; and his lifelong friend, Sister Monica. Serena had given them enough medication to last till Jimi could be taken to a hospital.

'How did you persuade Kuomi to let them go?' Serena asked Jake that evening.

'I appealed to him to imagine how Jimi's mother must be feeling, having already lost her husband, and not knowing whether her son was alive or dead. Mara did the rest.'

'Crafty devil!'

'It's called diplomacy. Any minute now, Kuomi's going to come asking about the radio.'

'I'd almost forgotten. What will you tell him?'

'I'll tell him it's almost fixed. It worked perfectly while I sent my message. There's just the matter of replacing a wire or two.'

'What will happen now?'

'The government troops are already on their way. My guess is that they'll pack the young rebels off home. Kuomi and a couple of others might have to face charges.'

'They won't shoot them?' Serena asked apprehensively.

'I doubt it. Here comes their leader now. Get everyone busy, clearing up or whatever, while I put the finishing touches to the radio, for Kuomi's benefit.'

'Consider it done. Good luck!'

The young soldiers couldn't have been more co-operative. The singing had put them in a mellow frame of mind. Serena was about to leave the hospital block to supervise the laundry when Mara cried out and then came rushing back.

No words were needed to understand Mara's delight. Abio was lying still, but his eyes were now open and he was gazing round in bewilderment. 'He live!' Mara cried with tears of joy.

Serena dismissed the others who

104

were crowding round and examined Abio. 'He'd be better off in hospital,' Serena told his mother gently.

'Kuomi say no hospital,' Mara replied dully.

'He may soon have no choice.'

The place was unusually quiet. After having a shower, Serena wandered into Father O'Leary's abandoned room. The beds were neatly made up, all sign of occupancy gone. She returned to her room, full of anxiety now that she and Jake were alone with the rebels.

Jake chose that moment to return, and suddenly the room was vibrant with life, the world a rosy place again. Whatever lay ahead, it didn't seem so bad with Jake beside her.

'What happened?' Serena asked him. 'Does Kuomi know the radio's working?'

'He knows all right, and as predicted, he's confiscated it.'

'Does it matter? I mean, you got the necessary message through, didn't you?'

'It matters. Once he tunes into the

nearest news station and hears the news in approximately . . . ' He consulted his watch. ' . . . half an hour, he'll know I sent that message and the balloon will go up.'

'And then?'

'We'll not be waiting to find out. We're getting out of here right now.'

'But it's getting dark, and we've no transport,' she objected, glancing out at the shadowy trees and remembering that predatory lioness with her spine-chilling roar.

'The best time,' he assured her. 'And we do have transport, of a kind. While you were all singing away and I was working on the radio, I had a visitor.'

'A visitor? Who?'

'Remember Buoni — the guy I mentioned who was supposed to be meeting us at the landing strip?'

'Yes, though of course I didn't actually meet him.'

'Well, he's been hanging about the mission, ready to come to our assistance if we got into real trouble.'

'Which we're about to! What does he suggest?'

'He showed me a motorbike in one of the outhouses. It's in good nick, with half a tank of petrol. It belongs to a young African doctor who was here when the uprising occurred. He used a four-wheel truck to drive the young nuns out of harm's way, leaving his bike behind. We're just going to have to borrow it and settle up with him at some point in the future.'

'It should be marvellous on this fine network of motorways,' she retorted acidly.

'It might not get us far, but it'll hopefully get us well on the way. Do you have a better idea?'

'No, I suppose not. Sorry, but it's an alarming prospect travelling out there in the dark on a two-wheeled vehicle.'

'You shouldn't damned well be here!'

'No need to keep reminding me.'

'I'm sorry. Let's not argue; it won't get us anywhere. We need to be out of here in the next half hour. That's when the news will be broadcast. I'm going to have a shower. My things are already packed. I suggest you pack what you need in a small rucksack, but only take the minimum.'

'There are bound to be young rebels hanging about in the courtyard. Won't they think it odd if we walk out of here complete with rucksacks?'

'I've thought of that. The bike's hidden in trees behind the mission. We'll have to climb out of the rear window. Think you can manage that? I've tried it — it's a bit of a squeeze, but it works.'

Serena studied the window. 'If you can get your shoulders through, I should have no problem.'

'It's not your shoulders I'm worried about.' He was grinning maddeningly.

'Don't be so adolescent!' she snapped.

He closed the gap between them, his hands closing round her shoulders. She looked up at him like a startled rabbit, trying to read the intent in the blue-green eyes.

'Adolescent, huh?' he murmured before subjecting her to a prolonged and thorough kiss.

It was impossible to define the emotions lurking in the depths of his eyes. Did she even want to? She dismissed them as pure lust. 'If you've quite finished,' she said tartly, 'I'll get on with my packing.'

'The bare minimum,' he warned, and disappeared into the bathroom. It was as though that kiss had never happened.

Serena packed some medical supplies along with a change of clothing or two, plus some sun cream and a paperback she was halfway through. She was struggling with the zip when Jake reappeared.

'What on earth are you doing?' he demanded, snatching the rucksack and, to her disbelief and fury, pulling out the contents. 'You call this the bare minimum?'

'Necessities,' she insisted.

He shook his head. 'It'll take a couple

of days to reach the border. We're not off on a long vacation. I'll pack what you need.'

She seethed with anger and embarrassment as his large hands picked over her belongings, discarding all but a few medical supplies, one shirt, one pair of socks and a change of underwear. No point in fighting him. He was probably right, she conceded, leaving him to shower and dress. She then pulled on her desert boots and tucked in her trouser bottoms.

They were similarly clad in clean khakis and a jacket. It was nearly dark, and the air felt pleasantly cool. It would be cold later on.

Jake looked her over. 'You'll do,' he said shortly.

So would he! He looked magnificently male, his broad shoulders narrowing to a taut belted waist and lean hips. His trousers were tucked into boots, like Serena's, to avoid picking up creepy-crawlies. His hair, now almost dry, flopped endearingly over his tanned face. He'd do for her any day.

Jake looked out of the window into the courtyard. Serena followed his gaze. Young soldiers had gathered round the well-head, chattering and laughing as they did every evening, more relaxed now than of late. How quickly things were about to change.

'Go and talk to them,' Jake told her.

'Wh-what? I thought we were about to leave.'

'We don't want them to realise that, though, do we? We need to appear as laid-back as they are.'

'You're not planning to do the dirty on me and take off alone, are you?'

'How could you even think it? Of course I'm not, you stupid woman. Just get out there and look relaxed. In five minutes' time the news will be broadcast. If Kuomi's listening, as he's sure to be, we mustn't let him find us.'

Serena wandered over to the well-head. As she got nearer, some of the men noticed her and turned to watch her, some grinning in a friendly fashion, some lecherously.

'You did well this afternoon,' she told them, making gestures she hoped conveyed her meaning. It occurred to her that a little extra noise right now could do no harm. 'You like to sing now?'

She launched into a popular song and they soon joined in. At the end of the first verse she heard Jake calling her. Looking round, she saw he was leaning nonchalantly against the door-jamb of their hut.

'Serena!' he called again and, with a decidedly possessive tone: 'Come here, wife.'

The singers heard, too, and watched her cross the yard to her 'husband', changing to more suggestive lyrics. Jake laughed and pulled her inside, firmly closing the door. Serena felt a thrill of what might have been, which was soon killed off by the laughter and catcalls outside.

'There's no doubt about what they

think we're getting up to,' Jake drawled as the singing resumed. 'Come on — I'll go first, then I'll catch you.'

He set a chair under the window. The transom window at the top through which they would have to escape was too high to reach from the floor. He switched off the light, leaving the room in darkness. Going through to the bedroom, he switched on a bedside lamp.

'More delaying tactics?' Serena guessed as he returned to the darkened room.

'Exactly. Now keep the window open as wide as you can.'

He climbed onto the chair and, having negotiated the space, was soon slithering to the ground.

'Well done!'

'Now pass me the bags.' Serena did so, then followed, with some difficulty. In the end she settled for a headlong exit with Jake grasping her waist and pulling her through.

'Let the window down slowly,' he

said. 'Don't trap your fingers.' He held her suspended while she quietly closed the window, then helped her find her footing.

'It's higher than I thought,' she said, somewhat breathless due to clambering through the window. Jake's proximity and the feeling of his supporting hands were imprinted on her body.

He strapped on her rucksack and swung his own into position, then took her hand to lead her through the undergrowth while her eyes became accustomed to the darkness. She glanced up nervously at the huge trees swaying all around them in the night breeze and shivered.

'Cold?' he asked solicitously.

'No. I guess someone walked over my grave or something.'

It wasn't cold as yet. The scorching heat of the day had diminished, but the night air still retained some warmth. He led her along unfamiliar pathways for some distance.

'I thought we were travelling by

motorbike,' Serena protested as the undergrowth caught at her clothes.

'So we are. Should I have announced our departure by parking the bike outside our hut? Come on. It's not far now.'

Several metres further on, Jake stopped beside a thicket and proceeded to delve into it, pushing the foliage aside. The moon, almost full, sailed clear of a bank of cloud at that moment to reveal the gleam of metal handlebars and a petrol tank. Before pulling the bike out, he picked up a rifle that lay beside it, and Serena wondered what kind of situation would require him to use it. She shuddered.

'Our young medic certainly took pride in his bike,' Jake commented. 'I checked it over as well as I could without starting the engine — just before I put their Jeep out of action. But in any case, Buoni assured me it was in perfect working order a few days ago. When we've finished with it, it might never be the same again.'

He had soon set it on the track, facing west. Then he took Serena's rucksack, put that and his own in the panniers, and secured the gun alongside. 'Hop on,' he said.

Serena threw one leg over the pillion seat while Jake climbed in front. 'Have you ridden pillion before?' he asked her.

'Occasionally, but I much prefer to be up front.'

'Now why doesn't that surprise me? First karate, now motorbikes! Another thing your brother coerced you into, I suppose. Well, you're out of luck — I'm in front.' He folded out the kick-start and rested his foot on it.

'I long ago decided that if I was going to hurtle along at death-defying speeds on a two-wheeled machine, I'd prefer to be the one in charge,' she persisted.

'Probably very wise with your brother,' he agreed complacently, and gunned the machine into life.

It worked first time, the loud roar echoing through the trees, no doubt reverberating round the mission. They would have a good start on Kuomi though, and with the remaining Jeep out of action, he and his men were now sitting ducks for government troops.

They roared off through the trees at breakneck speed. It was years since Serena had been on a bike, either as rider or pillion, and she had forgotten how alarming it could feel — even on smooth, tarmacked roads. Now they had to negotiate rough tracks more suited to the sturdiest of all-terrain vehicles. At least the track was quite wide at this point. From clinging to the back of her seat, as she would have done back home, Serena gave up the struggle and put her arms round Jake, clinging on for dear life.

From this position, she peered over his shoulder and watched the beam of the powerful headlight bounce off the tree trunks ahead. Above the roar of the engine, an occasional loud screech could be heard as some nocturnal creature was disturbed from its sleep, protesting into the night-dark jungle.

What had she let herself in for? Serena asked herself. Strangely, she felt no fear, only glorious exhilaration as she hugged Jake and settled her cheek against his broad back.

They were slowing down and Serena lifted her head to discover the reason. The track had narrowed and was now barely wide enough for the bike. It became increasingly rough, with deep potholes that Jake was doing his best to avoid. After a while there was an ominous thud as they hit a gully between two giant tree roots and came to an abrupt halt.

'Blast!' Jake exclaimed. 'That's it, I'm afraid. It was good while it lasted. From here, we go on foot.'

# 6

'You have to be joking! How come a Jeep can get through to the mission?'

'Perhaps by travelling a different route,' he suggested, matching scorn with sarcasm. 'We're heading for the border, which isn't far away. It'd be much further by road. I want us out of here before they make the Jeep roadworthy. Let's get these rucksacks on. I was hoping to make it over the hill. As it is, we may be grateful for shelter in one of the cave-like hollows in the hill itself.'

'It might already have an occupant,' Serena muttered.

'For God's sake, don't be so negative — and stand still while I fix this on.'

She tried not to react as he fixed her rucksack. He then shrugged into his own, strapping the rifle to it. By the light of a powerful torch he set off along the path, in his other hand an impressive kukri knife, shiny and deadly, ready to hack a way through the undergrowth. 'Stick as close to me as you can,' he told Serena. The rifle butt was clearly visible above his shoulder, ready to protect them both. She needed no further telling and remained one step behind him all the way.

They had almost reached the top of the hill when Jake stopped and shone the torch around them. The rocky formations to the right had openings which, to Serena's overactive imagination, looked like eyes. Jake ducked under an overhanging lip and slipped into the cave behind, flashing the torch around. 'This'll do,' he decided.

Serena followed apprehensively. Something fluttered past her head and she cried out, startled, clutching Jake's arm. Whatever it was hadn't actually touched her, but there had been a distinct draught as it passed.

'It was only a bat,' said Jake tersely. 'Don't tell me you're scared of them.'

'Of course not,' she said unconvincingly, clinging a little tighter to his arm. 'It was just unexpected.'

'How are you with creepy-crawlies?'

'Fine!' she lied airily. 'I'm not one of those pathetic women who get fazed by eight-legged beasties.'

'Which is why you don't call them by their proper name! It seems there's nothing more ominous than a bat colony inhabiting this place. We'll spend the night here.' He unrolled the blanket attached to his rucksack and proceeded to spread it on a flat area to one side of the cave. 'Your sleeping quarters, ma'am,' he announced with an exaggerated gesture of gallantry. And his, Serena guessed without needing to be told.

When she saw him strolling towards the entrance, she called, 'Where are you going?' She couldn't hide the alarm in her voice, as she was suddenly horrified at the prospect of spending the night alone.

'Don't worry, sweetheart,' Jake said with mock pleasantry. 'I'll be back.'

She wished she had kept her thoughts to herself when she realised Jake was outside the cave, gathering kindling and pieces of wood. He had soon started a blaze, sufficient to ward off any predator that happened along.

She had settled on the blanket, using her lumpy rucksack as a pillow, when Jake dropped down beside her. 'Here, try this for size,' he invited her, weighing up the situation and sliding an arm beneath her head.

It was bliss, although she would never admit it. Instead she released a little sigh, as if she was half-asleep and hardly aware of what was happening. The next moment she felt the brush of his lips on hers.

'Good night,' he whispered in the shadowy darkness, and she smiled contentedly.

★ ★ ★

Serena woke to find the sun slanting into the cave and an empty space beside her. Stretching and opening her eyes, she looked up at the roof of the cave. She sat up, shuddering in horror, for the entire roof was festooned with the most enormous cobwebs. She dreaded to think about the size of their occupants, or how far they might have travelled in the night.

A shadow cut off the light, and she jumped.

'Good morning,' came Jake's deep, familiar voice. 'Did you sleep well?'

'Surprisingly well,' she admitted, her eyes flickering towards the roof of the cave.

He laughed out loud. 'What a good thing you don't suffer from phobias.' Sinking to a crouching position, he handed her a mug. 'Coffee?'

She was amazed and delighted. 'How did you manage that?'

'By packing exactly what we needed and nothing more.' In spite of the reproach, he was clearly in excellent spirits.

'Mm, tastes wonderful.'

'I also helped myself to some bread, cheese and fruit from the kitchens. It's in a sealed container in my rucksack.' He stretched to a sitting position beside her and set some food between them. 'Help yourself.'

'Did you sleep well?' She nibbled alternatively at a roll and a piece of cheese as they sat companionably side by side. 'This is delicious, by the way.'

'I slept as well as I could in the circumstances.'

'Circumstances?'

'It was somewhat distracting with you wrapping yourself around me.' He didn't look up as he spoke, restraining a smile.

'I did not!' she denied hotly, a flush creeping up her cheeks.

'Afraid you did. I got up several times to replenish the fire and you welcomed me back quite delightfully.'

'Rubbish!'

She wondered, nevertheless, if it was true. If she acted like that in her sleep, how long would it take him to realise how she felt about him? She glanced up briefly, but the expression in the deep-set eyes was unreadable.

'When you're ready, we'll make a move,' he said. 'We'll make better headway before the sun reaches its zenith. I'm afraid there's no water for washing. We need it all for drinking.'

'That's okay. Here.' She produced two sealed wet wipes, handing him one of them and cleaning her hands and face with the other.

'Thanks.'

She stepped out into brilliant sunlight and a temperature now seventy-plus and climbing. 'Is there likely to be water on the way?' she asked with some concern.

'Bound to be. There's a whole chain of pools where the wildlife drink. We're on the edge of the jungle here, where trees meet savannah. Let's hope we're lucky.'

'Oh, just look, Jake.'

The cave was near the top of a hill, and the view from its opening was fabulous. Ranks of dark trees broke here and there to give distant glimpses of the vast plains of Africa, where giraffe, zebra and lions would be roaming — including that wounded lioness, if she was still alive.

'It's magnificent, isn't it?' Jake said. 'Maybe I'll bring you back here on safari one day — a camera safari.'

'Mm,' was all Serena could reply. Why did he have to say a stupid thing like that? Once they were back in England, she wouldn't see him for dust — as they both knew. Didn't they?

'The closest thing to a bathroom is a clump of bushes round the corner,' Jake informed her matter-of-factly. 'While you toddle off there, I'll douse the fire and pack up.'

An hour later they had made little headway, their progress hampered by dense, unyielding undergrowth that was even a challenge for Jake's kukri. Serena's clothes were sticking to her body. Perspiration ran down her back and between her breasts. The heat and

126

humidity were getting to her and she could hear her blood pounding in her ears. *Please don't let me pass out*, she prayed, sticking close to Jake.

Determined not to complain and give him cause to say *I told you so*, she plodded on. Her mouth felt dry as dust, her head ached and she was desperate for a drink, but pride kept her silent. It was maddening enough that he was doing the hard, physical job of hacking through the dense undergrowth; and yet, though like Serena he also had damp patches on his shirt, he didn't seem overcome by the intense heat.

He stopped suddenly and, with her eyes fixed on the ground, Serena cannoned into him. He twisted round. 'Christ!' he exclaimed. 'Why didn't you say something? Your face is as red as a lobster!'

'Sorry, I missed my appointment at the beauty parlour this morning,' she joked feebly.

'Don't be so bloody stupid, and stop being brave. Just look ahead.'

She peered through a haze of pain, ready to burst into tears at his sharp rebuke. The path ahead sloped downwards, and at the bottom lay the blue sparkle of water — clear, refreshing water trickling out of rocks to form a natural pool. 'Fantastic!' she breathed in relief. 'Just what this doctor ordered!'

As they drew nearer, they could see that the pool was set in a circle of rocks, broken only to display a view of the nearby savannah. A miniature waterfall splashed from a rocky overhang, forming a curtain over the broad ledge below.

'Like an oasis in the desert,' Serena declared. 'Did you leave the water-purifying tablets in my rucksack?'

'I did,' he replied and, looking contrite, he added 'They're still there. Thanks for reminding me — I was about to go and stand under that waterfall and drink my fill.' How tempting was that in this stifling heat? 'What a good thing I brought my own medic.'

'I'm not your own medic or anything else,' she reminded him acidly, but was perking up at the prospect of a drink.

'Just sit there and shut up,' he ordered pleasantly. 'I'll go and get you that drink.'

'Yes, sir,' she replied, sinking gratefully to the harsh brown earth close to the waterfall. She stretched out, covering her heated face with her hat and enjoying the pleasurable sound of cool, splashing water. Jake was soon beside her, raising her to a sitting position and holding a mug of treated water to her lips. It was surely the coldest, most welcome drink she had ever had — pure nectar.

'Wonderful!' she pronounced at last. 'Oh, wouldn't I just love a swim!'

'Why not? There's no sign of anything unpleasant in there. I'm certainly going in. We can leave our things on that ledge.'

The ledge was in a deep recess behind the waterfall. Jake set down their rucksacks and the rifle before proceeding to strip off his clothes quite unselfconsciously. Serena watched, fascinated. In her profession as a doctor she was quite familiar with the human body, but she'd never seen such a magnificent specimen. She glanced away when he was down to his boxer shorts; but rather to her relief, he kept them on. He was as perfect as a Grecian statue, but vibrant, alive, curiously vulnerable — and slimmer. She watched as he immersed himself in the pool and leapt around, cleaving through the still water and setting off ever widening ripples.

'It's quite shallow,' he called. 'Come on in.'

She envied him, splashing about, washing himself from head to toe while treading water, his black hair wetly following the lines of his shapely skull.

'It's wonderful! Come on!' he urged.

Serena's desperate desire to cool off battled with an innate sense of modesty. The latter won. 'No thanks. It's nice and cool here.'

'Don't be stupid. Get your damn clothes off and come for a swim, or I'll come over there and take them off myself!'

'Stop bossing me around, Jake.'

'I mean it, Serena. You'll feel a whole lot better if you cool off. For God's sake, you're the doctor — you should know what's best. Surely you're not too modest! Are you coming, or do I come and get you?'

'Stop ogling me and I will!' she yelled, furious at herself for being so ridiculously self-conscious.

She started to undress. Shoes, socks, trousers. Jake splashed around but then, satisfied that she was doing as he said, turned and swam away. Quickly she stripped off all but her briefs — she wasn't wearing a bra — and, before Jake turned, she was in the pool.

The water closed round her like silk and she swam rhythmically around, enjoying the luxury of feeling cool at last. What bliss! She flipped over to float on her back, closing her eyes against the

African sun. Something gripped her ankle and she shrieked. Jake chuckled beside her.

'You bastard! I thought it was a snake — of a different kind,' she amended nastily.

He raised his hands in a gesture of peace. 'Sorry,' he offered contritely.

His shoulders above the water were smooth and bronzed; his eyes full of warmth, devilment and so much more. Serena had never wanted him more. She swam away hastily, heading under the clear, cool water to extinguish the flare of desire.

She wanted him. She loved him. He wanted her, full stop. But once they returned to England, she would be just another number in his little black book, or the equivalent, if that. The knowledge gave her the strength to turn and swim back towards the waterfall. Using her discarded shirt as a towel, she wiped off the surplus water and wrapped it round her while she changed her underwear. Any remaining water would help to cool her body. She put on a clean shirt and, with her back to the pool, dragged a comb through her wet hair, smoothing out the tangles and squeezing out water. Jake hadn't followed her out; he clearly loved swimming. She cast a glance over her shoulder — and froze.

Jake had almost swum to the opposite bank before he turned. Behind him, the thick bushes that grew almost to the edge of the pool slid silently apart. A large yellow shape emerged and limped in an ungainly, lopsided fashion to the water's edge. Serena's thoughts sped to a scenario of the wounded lioness plucking the man she loved from the water and destroying his life right there before her eyes.

'No!'

She didn't know afterwards if she had voiced the syllable aloud or merely screamed it in her brain, but without pausing for thought, she grabbed the rifle that lay with Jake's discarded clothes, loaded in readiness for just such an emergency. Lifting it to her shoulder she took aim, her finger curling round the trigger. As she flicked it determinedly back, she was aware of Jake's hand lifting, shocked disbelief on his face for a brief instant before he took evasive action, leaping sideways.

The shot reverberated through the jungle. The lioness crumpled instantly, inches short of the pool, a neat hole between the eyes where the bullet that killed her had entered. Serena stood, the rifle at a sharp angle to the ground, shaking violently as Jake's dark figure emerged from the pool, approaching her warily. He was feet away when he suddenly lunged and grabbed the gun.

'You bloody stupid bitch!' he yelled furiously, to her astonishment and absolute terror. She had just saved his life, yet she had never seen him so angry. 'What the hell got into you? Would you rather see me dead and have to find your own way out of this jungle than risk getting close to another human being? I was only playing, for God's sake.'

Something in her expression stemmed the flow of words. 'Wh-what are you talking about, Jake?' she burbled, sinking to the flat rock before she fell. 'I killed . . . I killed . . . I've never killed . . . ' She raised a trembling arm towards the dead lioness.

Jake looked round and at last understood. 'My God, Serena — I thought you were trying to kill me!'

'Kill you?' she asked, startled. 'Why on earth should I want to kill you, when I . . . ' The confession of love lingered on her tongue but was never uttered. She suddenly became aware of Jake standing tall and strong, almost naked, rapidly drying in the heat; and herself, her shirt not yet buttoned, her breasts half-exposed. He could have been killed, his beautiful body horribly mutilated. Instead, he was here beside her, vibrantly alive. He dropped to the ground beside her and took her shaking body in his arms.

'You saved my life,' he said softly, his hands warm and soothing on her back. 'How can I ever thank you?'

'Oh Jake,' she murmured huskily. 'You didn't honestly think I . . . '

He lifted her chin, taking in her wounded eyes and soft, tremulous lips. 'I thought I'd annoyed you, scared you, whatever.' He kissed her temple.

'No, Jake,' she assured him softly. 'Of course I don't want to kill you. I . . . ' The air around them shimmered with sensations and unspoken thoughts. 'Look, do you mind putting some clothes on?'

He released her at once and stood up, pulling on a dry shirt before changing his wet boxer shorts for dry ones. Serena kept her back to him to give him some privacy while she dragged a comb through her hair.

Once they were both dressed, with trousers tucked into boots, they made a meal of their remaining supplies and refilled their water bottles. Neither felt like talking, deep in their own private thoughts. Having finished eating, they rinsed out the clothes they had been wearing and pinned them to their rucksacks to dry.

'Time to get back to reality,' Jake said. Serena's gaze wandered to the lifeless form of the lioness on the opposite bank. 'Look away,' he said. 'Let's get the hell out of here.'

# 7

Jake couldn't wait to get back to civilisation, Serena was convinced, where doubtless a string of attractive women would be vying for his attention. She could hardly blame him for taking advantage of that. She knew she was something of an anachronism. Serena wanted commitment, not just a physical relationship. She wanted the lot: trust, caring, stability. Jake offered none of these.

They pressed on, refreshed by the cool swim and scratched meal. As the trees started to thin, the heat increased in intensity. At least there was less undergrowth to be hacked away. Serena was glad of that for Jake's sake. He must be feeling as weary and lethargic as she was, with her clothes sticking uncomfortably to her body. They kept going, barely speaking, but it was not an uncomfortable silence. They did seem more at ease with each other.

Once back in England, Jake would probably put this trip and everything connected with it out of his mind. He was used to working in the warring hotspots of the world, so it was probably nothing out of the ordinary for him. He would soon forget Serena, never realising that beneath her cool exterior she was a writhing mass of emotion. She, on the other hand, would always remember Jake Andrews. He would be there in the deeper recesses of her mind to the end of her days.

'Are you all right, sweetheart?' His sudden enquiry and unexpected endearment broke into her thoughts as he turned to face her.

'I'm fine,' she assured him, loving him with her eyes.

'Not much further now, if I've calculated correctly.'

He was right. The trees were now much more spaced out, revealing wide pathways indented with the tracks of recent traffic. Jake dropped back to walk beside her as soon as it was possible, and took her hand. 'Serena, you've been wonderful, do you know that? Right through this entire ghastly episode.'

Her heart turned a somersault. Praise from the hyper-critical Jake Andrews? 'Not sorry I came then?'

'I didn't say that,' he replied darkly, causing a stab of disappointment. 'But there have certainly been moments.'

'Glad to have been of use,' she said drily.

'That, too.' He paused. 'You were really upset about the lioness, weren't you?'

'I'm trained to save life, not to kill.'

'She was dying, Serena. You did her a favour.'

'That's one way of looking at it.' And it made her feel a whole lot better.

'Where on earth did you learn to shoot like that?'

'Chris and I used to go clay-pigeon shooting. But I never expected to point a gun at a living creature.'

'She was horribly wounded,' he reminded her. 'You saved her from a long and agonising death, love.'

The 'love' a taxi-driver might call you. A bandage to salve her tortured thoughts, to take her mind off the lioness.

'What did your parents think of their daughter riding motorbikes, shooting and doing karate with Chris?'

'I doubt they had any idea.' Serena couldn't suppress a chuckle.

'How come?'

'They were very distant as parents. They left us in the care of paid staff while they pursued their own interests. Daddy was the hunting, shooting, fishing type. Mummy's life revolved around the social calendar.'

'Ascot? Wimbledon?'

'Right. Mummy's terribly vague, though I sometimes wonder if it's all a facade to please Daddy.'

'It would irritate me.'

'Horses for courses, I suppose. Daddy thinks women are pretty ornaments, and

Mummy is very pretty. I don't know why they had us children, though. They never showed any warmth towards us.'

'Did that bother you?'

Serena was saved from answering. The trees had just petered out and in the dry, dusty space in front of them soldiers were standing around in scattered groups. Serena hesitated but Jake strode boldly forward, urging her to keep pace beside him. 'It's all right — they're government troops.' With guns, was Serena's first thought, but she was soon reassured.

A colonel in a neatly pressed uniform with smart epaulettes and a multitude of decorations spotted them and walked towards them, arms outstretched and a welcoming smile on his face. 'Mr and Mrs Andrews, I presume?'

'Right,' agreed Jake. Lengthy explanations were too complicated, though Serena half-wondered what it would be like if it were true.

'We've been watching out for you along the jungle perimeter.' A soldier in a Jeep was engaged in transmitting a message. 'We were about to send in search parties. You've saved us a lot of time and trouble, so thank you.'

'Don't mention it,' Jake said. 'What happened to the rebels?'

'All rounded up. Young idiots — just one ambitious but foolish man and a bunch of kids, virtually. The leader's son and a couple of others have been taken to hospital. Father O'Leary and Sister Monica got the injured boy home. They're off to Ireland for an extended leave but will be returning to the mission.'

'I didn't imagine they'd retire,' said Jake.

'Now we have a wounded lioness to track down before she does any more harm.'

'She's dead.'

'You shot her, Mr Andrews?'

'No, my wife did, and saved my life into the bargain.'

'Good heavens, you must be very proud of her.'

'You can't imagine how much.'

Things happened very quickly after that. First they were taken to a hotel for a much-needed shower and change of clothes. After a delicious meal, they were whisked to the airport in time to catch a late plane home.

Serena was so tired that she slept most of the way back. She awoke disoriented, realising they were both wearing sweaters and jeans — so normal, so unlike their desert gear. Their sojourn in Africa took on the nature of a dream, a fantasy totally divorced from real life. She glanced up to meet Jake's watchful eyes.

'Back to civilisation, hmm?' His voice, so matter-of-fact and devoid of emotion, plunged an invisible knife into her heart.

'Absolutely,' she agreed bravely. 'I was just thinking so myself. It all seems like a dream now — or rather a nightmare,' she tacked on carelessly, crying inside.

His expression hardened; the knife

twisted. 'Don't you agree?' she asked with feigned nonchalance.

He shrugged. 'It might make good copy for my next book,' he replied with a levity to match her own, his eyes not quite meeting hers.

'Which bits in particular?' she persisted with studied coolness.

'Whatever fits the story, I suppose,' he replied dismissively.

Through the window she could see lights twinkling below. Everything was growing nearer, more distinct. The approach lights of Heathrow came into view and their plane banked, lining up for touchdown.

Serena forced herself to concentrate on the reality around them — the clunk of seatbelts being fastened; the cry of a small child feeling the change of pressure in its ears. She tried to block out the thoughts gnawing at her consciousness. Surely there were some moments Jake would cherish and wish to keep private? Was the experience they'd shared just copy for his next book? How would he portray her, if at all? Like some frightened little virgin, too scared of getting hurt to dip her toes in the waters of life?

No, of course not. He would just use the background and maybe some of the incidents relating to the revolt they'd witnessed. After all, wasn't Jake just as scared of living as she was when commitment was involved?

'When do you expect to hear about the job you applied for?' he asked as the wheels touched the runway, rumbling noisily as the brakes were applied and the plane gradually screamed to a halt.

'I expect a letter will be waiting for me at the flat.'

'Dorset will be quite a change from London.'

'A pleasant one, and certainly more pleasant than the depths of darkest Africa,' she forced herself to reply, her voice distinctly prickly.

'Then I hope you get it,' he wished her icily.

Any hopes Serena might have entertained of crawling away to lick her wounds in private were quickly dashed. The darkened tarmac erupted in a battery of flashbulbs as they emerged from the plane. 'Hell and damnation!' Jake swore, clearly as anxious as Serena to distance himself from their shared experience. 'Your dear brother has laid on the red carpet treatment.'

They were hurried into the VIP lounge, where Chris was waiting along with what seemed like half a million reporters. 'Never thought my little sister would be so famous,' he quipped cheerfully.

'I'll kill you for this, Chris,' she fumed.

'Let's get this circus over and get the hell out of here,' Jake growled, at least in agreement with her on this point.

Neither, it seemed, could wait to see the back of each other. It was impossible, though, to avoid the barrage of questions about what had happened in Africa, how the mini-revolution had started, what had happened to those at the mission, and how it had eventually been resolved. It had clearly grown out of all proportion on the news scene, and there was a certain disappointment when the truth emerged.

Serena breathed a sigh of relief. But then, when she thought there were no more questions to answer, the familiar grating voice of a female newshound demanded: 'Is it true you two got married out in Africa?'

'You'll have to wait for the announcement,' Jake replied with a grin, but a quick glance told Serena he was furious about being romantically linked to her in public. 'But don't hold your breath.'

'Is that a yes?'

'Come on, that's it,' said Jake grimly, standing up.

'You can tell me all about it later,' said a bemused Chris. 'The wretched woman got an exclusive with Father O'Leary, and priests don't lie — or do they?'

Chris shepherded his sister through

the throng. They soon became separated from Jake. Serena glanced back for one last glimpse of the man she had fallen in love with. Case in hand, he had managed to shake off the crowd and was striding towards the exit when the sylph-like figure of a leggy brunette hurtled towards him, a curtain of shiny black hair swinging about her shoulders.

'Jake!' she called with transparent delight.

'Sophie!'

Serena read the name on his lips. She watched, dark misery in her heart, as the brunette was swept laughing into his embrace.

'Do you want to wait for Jake?' asked Chris, not witnessing the tender reunion.

'He's already left. I saw him go, and I never want to set eyes on the swine again.'

'So there was no marriage? Or it was one of the shortest on record. Come on, I've booked you into a hotel.'

'Thanks. I don't want to go back to the flat yet. I need to have a serious talk with Debbie about Simon, but I can't face that problem right now. I just want a long sleep. I think I'll get out of London even if I don't get that job.'

'Don't decide yet, love. Have a couple of nights' rest before you decide anything. Okay?'

'I guess so.'

Chris drew up outside a luxury hotel in the heart of London. 'A treat on the firm,' he told her as they crossed the lobby. 'Your cheque will be arriving in a few days, and it'll be a large one.'

Serena couldn't care less. She completed the formalities of signing in and turned to her brother. 'I'm going straight up, Chris, if you don't mind. I just need to sleep. Thanks for meeting me. Just one thing.'

'Anything, sis.'

'You haven't booked Jake in here, have you?'

'Good lord, no. The man likes to make his own arrangements.'

She could guess why. 'Promise you won't tell him where to find me, either now or later.'

'But what about . . . ?'

'Promise, Chris. Dammit, it's the least you can do. You set me up to face guns, wild animals and the despicable Jake Andrews.'

'As bad as that, eh? What on earth happened between you?'

'Never mind. You haven't promised.'

'Are you sure this is what you want?'

'Positive! Why do you think I'm insisting?'

'Okay, you've got it. I'll see you later.' He looked at his watch. 'It's eight o'clock already. I'm off for breakfast. See you about tea-time. We'll talk then.'

That meant he would try to bully her into talking. He had despatched her and Jake out to Africa to get a story, albeit in the guise of a rescue mission, and he wouldn't be happy till he knew every last detail. In spite of the press conference at the airport, once he knew the facts he would create a marvellous programme. He always did. He would use archive film of the mission, or send cameramen out there now that peace was restored. Maybe Jake would front the programme — but they could jolly well do without her!

After showering and eating the light meal which she'd had delivered by room service, Serena crawled between the linen sheets of the enormous bed and revelled in its size and comfort. Sleep eluded her, her mind still teeming with thoughts of Jake.

He was an utter and complete swine where women were concerned, only interested in his own gratification. That poor brunette. She looked young and fresh and thoroughly likable, if Serena were honest. She was clearly dotty about Jake, and just as clearly heading for heartbreak.

Her thoughts rambled on, and she had to admit there was another side to Jake. He had appointed himself her protector, even though he hadn't wanted to take her in the first place. He certainly hadn't failed her in that role, even though their escape through the jungle had been no sinecure.

He wanted his freedom — that was for sure. He wanted sex without commitment, and that was something Serena could never agree to. When he had kissed her, she had wanted so much more, so had she been wrong to hold back? Now all she was left with was memories of Jake. In the long, lonely years ahead, all men would be measured by the yardstick of Jake Andrews — and found wanting.

She might as well get used to it. It was clear he only wanted Serena when no one else was around. As soon as he'd returned, he was claimed by the beautiful Sophie. A sob rose in Serena's throat as she recalled the look of love on Jake's face when he swept the brunette into his arms.

She finally dozed, though fitfully. By early afternoon she was wide awake. Deciding she couldn't face Chris and his interrogation, she knew there was nothing for it but to leave.

First she phoned the Dorset hospital to inform them she had returned from abroad but would not be at the flat to receive letters. The hospital administrator reluctantly agreed to fax a copy of their letter to the hotel. She had got the job!

Why did she not feel ecstatic? It felt like an anticlimax after the African adventure, but she was quietly pleased. She collected her belongings and went down to check out.

'Is anything wrong, Dr Blake?' asked the manager. 'Your brother booked the room for several days. If there's anything we can do . . . '

'There's nothing wrong,' she quickly assured him. 'I've just changed my plans, that's all.'

They called her a taxi to take her to Waterloo. She would sort out Debbie and the flat later. She just had to get away from London, and the green acres of southern England seemed highly attractive right now.

Her first priority was to sort out accommodation. She had always loved the New Forest, just over the county border from the hospital where she would be working. That was where she would concentrate her search.

It was early evening by the time she arrived in Lyndhurst, a delightful town in the heart of the New Forest. Tomorrow would be soon enough to go round the local estate agents. Meanwhile, she booked into an ancient-looking hotel right in the heart of the little town.

'We've only the one room left, but I think you'll like it.'

Serena followed Mrs Woods, the landlady, up a rickety staircase and along the uneven floor of a dark wood-panelled corridor that had never known a spirit level. She opened the door to a room decorated in blue and white, with a bowl of bright yellow dahlias on a chest of drawers.

'It's delightful,' said Serena. 'I'll take it.'

The ancient four-poster had probably been the setting for many a romantic encounter. No, she must stop thinking along those lines. She must concentrate on practical thoughts.

She switched the television on and settled back against the whiter-than-white, lavender-scented bedding, to watch the news. First, the political scene at home with the latest sleaze report. Conflict in the Middle East. Refugees and asylum seekers on the move. Next, to Serena's horror, her own face next to Jake's as they faced a rash of reporters at that wretched news conference.

Jake looked devastating — big, handsome and self-possessed, fielding every question with confidence. To her own eyes, Serena looked bemused, unused to publicity as she was. Yet, as she answered questions relating to her patients, she matched up to any professional discussing her work.

'Is it true the two of you got married out in Africa?' came that unnerving

Cockney demand.

Would the average viewer catch the flare of anger in Jake's eyes, or the shocked horror of her own expression? How would Jake explain to his lady love? Without the slightest difficulty, no doubt, practised charmer that he was.

There was a knock on the door. 'Come in!' she called.

Mrs Woods glanced at the television. 'Excuse me, Dr Blake, but we've just seen the news, and I'd like to reassure you that you can rely on our absolute discretion.'

'Thank you, Mrs Woods. I would prefer that no one knows I'm staying here.'

'Would you like your meals sent up?'

'That would be wonderful for the time being. I am still Dr Blake, by the way, not Mrs Andrews.'

Mrs Woods smiled. 'That's entirely your business, my dear. He is handsome, though, isn't he?'

★ ★ ★

It was a balmy summer evening, so Serena went for a walk, mingling with the tourists, wearing dark glasses as a disguise. The ancient town was delightful, as were its surroundings. She reached the edge of town where the New Forest began. Yes, she would love it here, away from the noise and traffic fumes of London.

# 8

The following morning Serena headed for an estate agent, Goldsmiths, recommended by her landlady. She knew what she was looking for.

'I'd like to find a cottage with about half an acre of land,' she told Ralph Goldsmith. He was the proprietor of the agency and looked like the typical estate agent: smart suit, toning shirt and tie, neat haircut, and aged around thirty-five. 'It doesn't matter if it's a bit rundown. I enjoy a bit of DIY. Nothing structural, mind you.'

By lunchtime they had visited several properties, none of which were quite right. Serena made a mental note to buy a car the very next day. She would enjoy driving round the area to see what she could find.

'That's all we have on our books at the moment, but don't despair — new properties are coming on the market all the time. Although they're soon snapped up, especially if they're in need of repair. They're cheaper, which most people soon cotton on to.'

'That's a pity.'

'I'm sorry I can't help for the moment, but we have some nice properties for rental if you would like a temporary solution.'

'I don't have much choice. I can't stay at the hotel indefinitely. My job starts imminently, so the sooner I'm settled, the better. I'd prefer to buy in the New Forest, but I'll look around Bournemouth, too.'

Ralph Goldsmith scratched his balding head. 'You could always take Briar Cottage for the winter.'

'Briar Cottage?'

'It's a holiday cottage that's usually vacant for most of the winter. I've got the details in the office.'

'I'd like to see them.'

Back in the office she read the details. Her hopes soared. 'Let's go take a look,' she said.

Briar Cottage was as pretty as its name suggested. It had two rooms upstairs and two down, a kitchen-diner and a modern bathroom. The small but colourful garden was enclosed by a white picket fence that separated the garden from the forest outside and kept out the cattle and horses roaming free there.

A mare with its foal was grazing nearby, thrown into relief by the setting sun. It wasn't the sort of place she had envisaged buying, but for now it would be perfect — well away from the intrusive eyes of the press.

'It's available until May,' the agent explained, 'but there'd be no problem re-letting if you found something you wanted to buy during that time.'

'It's beautiful.' She looked around the comfortable sitting room and out of the window at the glorious surroundings. 'I'll take it,' she decided.

Serena moved in and, although the cottage was in good condition, she spent the next few days cleaning it from top to bottom to make it her own. She also stocked the pantry, fridge and freezer. Her clothes and most of her belongings were in the London flat, but she was reluctant to contact Debbie to get her to send them on. Instead, she took a train to Southampton, returning in the small but sturdy car she bought there with her purchases of jeans, shirts and sweaters and a light but warm down anorak. She still felt the cold after the heat of Africa.

The utilities were all connected at the cottage, and Ralph Goldsmith offered to make the changeover from the previous tenants, leaving Serena to enjoy a life for the time being without stress and without routine. Of course that would change soon enough once she started work.

Inevitably, life adopted a pattern. Serena spent the mornings on domestic chores, then drove into Lyndhurst to do a bit of shopping and have a coffee. People started to say good morning and, if anyone remembered that short television interview, it soon became a nine days' wonder, quickly forgotten.

In the afternoons, when the weather was good, she went for a hike through the forest, where she met others out walking with dogs or children. Some were riding horseback, something she and her brother used to enjoy, and she decided she would choose a property with stabling and buy herself a horse. In the evenings she cooked herself a light but nourishing meal and then settled down to read or listen to music. She enjoyed historical romances but also read medical journals to keep up to date.

Though Serena tried to keep her thoughts focused, she found them straying all too often to her recent adventure. At sunset the sky would take on a myriad of brilliant hues, but her mind would wander to the times she and Jake had watched this same sun setting over a dramatic African landscape.

Was Jake watching now, perhaps at his hideaway in Provence, as the sun sank into an indigo mist or melted into a pool of crimson before disappearing beneath the horizon? Was he alone, or with the beautiful brunette? Or someone maybe more sophisticated and less likely to get hurt?

Serena would sometimes wake in the night and wonder if she had been wrong to deny him. At least then she would have memories of his loving. Or lusting, rather.

*   *   *

After a fortnight at the cottage, she could no longer put off calling Debbie.

'Serena! Where in the world have you been? I've got the media practically camped on my doorstep. And as for that brother of yours . . . And Jake Andrews!'

'Jake?' Serena went rapidly from hot to cold. 'What did he want?'

'You, I imagine. He didn't say, but I

164

tell you this — he's one helluva mad guy. He turns up several times a day, convinced I'm hiding you in a cupboard. Just give me your landline number and get him off my back, for pity's sake.'

'I didn't phone to talk about Jake Andrews, or my brother, for that matter. I want us to sort out the flat.'

'It's sorted. A girl from work wants to move in. I was just waiting to hear from you and get your approval.'

'What about Simon? Does she know about him?'

'Oh, he's history. I soon realised what a creep he was. I've met someone at the gym who does something clever at the Stock Exchange.'

'Doesn't sound like your usual type. What's his name?'

'Jeremy — you'd approve. Anyway, when are you coming to get your stuff? And what about the furniture?'

'You can keep the furniture. Most of it's second-hand. Sell it if you need the space, or give it to a charity shop. Do you think you could pack up my clothes and other bits and pieces and send them on? I shan't be coming up to London yet.'

'Sure. Would your reluctance have anything to do with the gorgeous Jake Andrews?'

'In a way. The thing is, I don't want Jake or my brother to know my whereabouts. Can you deal with the landlord? You need to get a new lease drawn up, removing my name. I'll sign anything necessary.'

'No problem.'

'I'll pay my share of the bills to the end of the lease. If I give you my address, will you promise not to pass it on to *anyone*?'

'Trust me. But Jake is like a dog with a bone, gnawing away till he gets what he wants — and I think what he wants is you!'

If that was so, it was only as a member of his personal harem! Maybe he was just mad as fire because Serena wouldn't be available for Chris's documentary, to corroborate his story and add the feminine touch.

'But you promise not to tell him or Chris?'

'Yes, of . . . oh golly, there goes the doorbell. Guess who?' Serena could imagine Debbie screwing her eyes up to make out the caller through the frosted glass. 'Quick, give me your phone number.'

Serena did so, adding, 'Don't leave it there where he could see it.'

'It's okay. I've torn it off and put it in my pocket. I'll call you.'

So he was there, in her flat, with Debbie. Serena could almost feel his presence through the phone in her hand. How fanciful, she chided herself. Thank goodness she could trust Debbie.

She felt particularly restless that night, so the following morning she drove into Lyndhurst to mingle with the crowds. She didn't want to be alone — it left too much time to think.

She'd soon finished her shopping,

and was just contemplating where to go for a coffee when someone called her name. Turning, she saw the helpful estate agent, Ralph Goldsmith.

'Dr Blake, how nice to see you. I've been meaning to call to see how you're getting on. Are you settling in all right?'

'I'm fine, Mr Goldsmith, and I'm delighted with Briar Cottage.'

'Do call me Ralph. Everyone does.'

'Ralph, then.'

'Have you got time for a coffee?'

'Funnily enough, I was just wondering where to get one. There are so many lovely little cafés in Lyndhurst.'

'My treat, then. This place is one of the best for decent coffee.'

Serena immediately regretted accepting. She'd become selfish with her time and now wanted to get back to her bolt hole. Ralph had been helpful though, and could be again while she looked for a more permanent home, so she'd do well to stay friendly. 'This place' was the hotel where she had stayed when she had first arrived in Lyndhurst. With a hand at her elbow, he escorted her inside.

A partially glazed screen separated the coffee lounge from the foyer. Mrs Woods smiled her approval seeing them together. The coffee was excellent, but Serena didn't want people getting the wrong idea. She had no desire whatsoever to get to know Ralph any better. Jake had spoilt her for pleasant but ordinary individuals like Ralph.

'You were right about the coffee,' she said. 'It's very good. Have you always lived locally?'

'More or less. I have family all over the area.'

He went on to elaborate, but Serena was only half-listening. She was facing the foyer, which was clearly visible through the glazed screen. The street door suddenly whooshed open and a large man, radiating energy, shot into the hotel.

Serena paled. Had she conjured him up out of the ether? It wasn't possible! Debbie had promised! Yet there he was, huge and handsome. She felt breathless. Her heart set up a staccato rhythm in her chest.

'I say, are you all right? You've gone awfully pale,' said Ralph.

'I'm fine,' Serena assured him shakily, shrinking in her seat in the hope of becoming invisible to Jake.

He was standing with his back to her, talking to Mrs Woods at the reception desk. She produced the register and he took out a pen as if to sign, but she knew it was a ploy to scan recent guests. He only had to turn round to catch sight of her silver-blond hair gleaming in the finger of sunlight pointing through the window.

'Can I get you a brandy?' Ralph asked.

'No, really, I . . . '

Perhaps she could escape into the ladies'. Mrs Woods was shaking her head ruefully, but her eyes darted nervously in Serena's direction. Jake suddenly swung round, following her gaze, and speared Serena with his eyes.

The next moment he was loping towards their table, large and menacing, fury all over his face.

'There you are, my dear,' he said with mock pleasantry.

'What do you want, Jake?'

'I think our little tiff has gone on long enough, my love,' he went on, clearly for Ralph's benefit. 'Won't you introduce me to your friend?'

'Ralph Goldsmith, the agent who found me somewhere to rent,' she explained, but did not complete the introduction.

'I hope you'll be able to re-let, Ralph. My wife will be moving out as of today,' he informed the bemused estate agent.

'Your wife? I didn't know. Serena, you don't have to go with this man,' Ralph told her, sensing all was not well. 'If he's been ill-treating you, even if he is your husband . . . '

'Butt out, Goldsmith,' Jake snapped nastily.

'It's all right, Ralph. He's not violent.'

'Whereas my wife is a dab hand at karate, and no mean shot either,' Jake informed a goggle-eyed Ralph.

Jake may not have been violent until then, but at that moment he looked ready to commit murder. Whatever he had to say, though, Serena had no intention of hearing it in front of strangers. She stood up and picked up her parcels.

'I'll take those,' said Jake, seizing the parcels in one hand and grasping her elbow with the other.

'Where do you think you're taking me?' she demanded as he marched her along the narrow street and round the corner to the car park, not stopping until they were standing beside a gleaming black XJS.

'Get in,' he ordered.

'I've got my own car.'

'We'll collect it later. We've got to talk, so be a good girl and get in.'

She was seething at being addressed like a naughty child as he opened the door and thrust her inside. In a few strides he was at the driver's door and, after flinging the parcels in the back, he climbed in.

'We'll go to your place,' he decided. 'Direct me, will you?'

Wearily, Serena obeyed. Why fight him? He was probably used to getting his own way and resented not getting her! They soon reached the cottage, where he parked the car — like him, big, dark and menacing.

'Very nice! A little love-nest for you and Ralphie, eh?'

'Don't be ridiculous! I hardly know the man!'

'You hardly knew me, but we spent several nights sharing the same room.'

'Only the room,' she reminded him.

'And a blanket in a cave.'

'Desperation,' she retorted acidly.

'You should have made that plainer.' He smirked, deliberately misunderstanding.

'I didn't mean — '

'I could do with a coffee. I've been up since dawn. I'd have driven down last night but I thought it would be easier to find you today. I didn't realise how easy it would be.'

'How did you find me?' She went through to the kitchen and set the coffee machine going. 'Debbie was the only one who had my phone number, and she promised not to pass it on.'

Jake lounged in the doorway. The kitchen shrank, and despite herself she felt a thrill that he was there in her home, so gorgeous, so desirable. She mustn't think like that, though. She wanted exclusivity, and that he would never agree to.

'She didn't,' he said. 'Well, not exactly.'

'What does that mean?'

'I saw part of your name on the torn-off page of the phone pad. While she went off to make some coffee I paused to tie my shoelace and grabbed the page underneath. The impression of your number was quite clear. It's a trick I've used in one of my novels,' he said smugly.

'Very clever.'

'The post code gave me Lyndhurst; and the rest, as they say, is history.'

How simple he made it sound. How did anyone ever manage to disappear? She picked up the coffee tray.

'Let me take that,' he insisted. 'This way?'

'It's difficult to get lost,' she retorted drily, as he headed for the sitting room.

'Come and sit beside me,' he ordered, setting the tray down on the low table in front of the settee.

Serena complied, refusing to be intimidated in her own home but leaving a space between her own legs and his long, muscular thighs. 'Why are you here, Jake? You don't need me for Chris's programme.'

'Not necessarily, no. Mind you, a woman's viewpoint always adds an interesting dimension.'

'Then why?'

He swung round and jerked her into his arms, tipping her chin to force her to look up at him. 'I came for you, of course. We belong together, you and I.' His voice took on a raw, husky quality. 'I enjoyed playing husband and wife out in Africa. I'm not ready to end it, not yet.'

'D-don't be ridiculous,' she stammered, but his lips silenced hers. It was so wonderful to be in his arms again that Serena nearly lost track of reality. Her arms found their way round his neck, her fingers toying with the thick, soft hair at his nape.

'I'd forgotten just how beautiful you are,' he murmured against her throat. 'I fancied you to death the moment I set eyes on you.'

Fancied? Those alarm bells were ringing again. This was Jake Andrews, who shied away from commitment. The Jake Andrews who arrived back in England and rushed straight into the arms of another woman. She struggled free and reached for the coffee pot. 'Black, no sugar, I believe?'

'Nice of you to remember. What the devil's wrong, Serena? I thought we

176

were getting close and then you went cold on me.'

'I suddenly realised what a louse you are.' She picked up her cup and held it as a shield.

'Meaning?'

'Look, I know what you want, but let's face it — your writing career keeps you mainly in the south of France. My job, the one I really wanted, keeps me here in England. Let's be sensible — I don't want a messy relationship to put a spanner in the works, for either of us.'

He took the cup from her fingers and put it with his on the table. 'Let's *not* be sensible, Serena. Let's be truly *un*sensible. Let's get married and live in a delightful manor house I've found not far from here.' He reached for her again but she slid away and stood up, hands on hips, facing him.

'Why on earth would I want to marry you, Jake Andrews?' she demanded, when what she really wanted to know was why on earth *he* would want to marry *her*! She loved him, which was a good reason for her; but he, on the other hand, had made it clear that he only fancied her. That was not sufficient reason for what was, to her, a lifetime commitment.

He stood up slowly and closed the distance between them, his arm sliding round her middle, drawing her in.

'I want to marry you so that you are there in the mornings, when I wake; I want you there to brighten my days; to offer warmth and comfort at night.' He gathered her even closer and tilted her chin, refusing to let her look away, mesmerising her with the heavenly blue-green of his eyes. 'To bear my children and, in general, share my life, so that when we're old we'll have a fund of wonderful shared memories to recount to our grandchildren.'

It sounded blissful, almost too blissful. She felt the sting of tears behind her eyes and thought she would melt under the warmth of his gaze. Why did he have to sound so sweet, so romantic, so sincere? 'But you don't believe in commitment, Jake. And what about Sophie?' she demanded, getting to the nub of the matter.

'I didn't believe in commitment, if we're talking marriage, before I met you. One look at you and my world shifted on its axis. I fell for you hook, line and sinker.' He really did sound sincere.

'And Sophie?' she persisted.

He ignored her question. 'I decided years ago not to allow myself the luxury of loving someone to distraction. My parents were deeply in love to the end, almost to the exclusion of anyone else.'

'They presumably loved their children.'

His bleak expression told her otherwise.

'How did it end?'

'We were on a sailing holiday in the Aegean. There was a freak storm and the yacht capsized. My father tried desperately to save my mother. I managed to grab my young sister and help her to cling to some wreckage.

Then we watched helplessly as our parents perished. They left us enough for me to finish my education and for my sister to go to boarding school. I looked after her till she embarked on a career.'

'What does she do?'

'She's a history lecturer at a uni in Surrey and is engaged to another lecturer, a widower with two children. When they get married, which will be soon, we shall sell the family home and I shall buy the manor house down here. It's near enough to your hospital and quiet enough for me to write. It's also large enough for children, dogs, horses . . . '

It sounded idyllic. 'I couldn't marry without love, Jake.'

His eyes clouded. 'Have I misread the signs? I rather hoped you did love me.'

She looked away, but he turned her face back. She couldn't dissimulate. Her love was shining in her eyes, clear and unmistakable.

'As I said, I hoped you loved me,

since I've fallen hopelessly in love with you and can't imagine life — '

'You've what?'

'I love you, Serena and, as I said, I hoped — '

'I do love you, Jake, but I'm not prepared to share my husband with the delectable Sophie.'

'Why not?' Then the truth dawned. 'You saw Sophie at the airport?' She nodded unhappily. 'Darling girl, I thought I'd explained. Sophie is my sister, the girl who gave me this signet ring.' He ran his thumb over the ring. 'I hope the two of you will get on, since I'm very fond of her.'

'Your sister?'

'My sister!'

'Oh Jake, I feel so stupid.'

'And you'll marry me?' There was a trace of uncertainty in his beautiful eyes.

'Oh yes, Jake. I'll marry you. Yes, yes, yes.'

'I don't know what else you're agreeing to, but let's go and fix up the ceremony before you change your mind.'

Serena could only murmur her assent against his descending lips.

We do hope that you have enjoyed reading this large print book.

Did you know that all of our titles are available for purchase?

We publish a wide range of high quality large print books including:
**Romances, Mysteries, Classics**
**General Fiction**
**Non Fiction and Westerns**

Special interest titles available in large print are:
**The Little Oxford Dictionary**
**Music Book, Song Book**
**Hymn Book, Service Book**

Also available from us courtesy of Oxford University Press:
**Young Readers' Dictionary**
**(large print edition)**
**Young Readers' Thesaurus**
**(large print edition)**

For further information or a free brochure, please contact us at:
**Ulverscroft Large Print Books Ltd.,**
**The Green, Bradgate Road, Anstey,**
**Leicester, LE7 7FU, England.**
**Tel:** (00 44) **0116 236 4325**
**Fax:** (00 44) **0116 234 0205**

# A MOMENT LIKE THIS

## Rena George

When Jenna Maitland's cousin Joss flees the responsibilities of their family's department store empire in Yorkshire, he escapes to Cornwall to follow his true calling and paint. Accompanied by the mysterious Gil Ryder, Jenna sets off south to find him. Once in Cornwall, Jenna finds herself becoming increasingly attracted to Gil — but is warned off by the attractive Victoria Symington, who appears to regard Gil as her own. Meanwhile, Joss's whereabouts has been discovered — but he is refusing to return . . .

# BROKEN PROMISES

## Chrissie Loveday

The greatest day of Carolyn's life has arrived: she is to marry her beloved Henry. But when she gets to the church, it becomes clear that something is terribly wrong. The groom has disappeared! Devastated, Carolyn is supported by her brother and his girlfriend as she tries to pick up the pieces of her life. When she meets kind, caring Jed, she feels as if she really is over Henry — but is this just a rebound? And will she ever find out why she was jilted at the altar?

# HER HIGHLAND LAIRD

## Carol MacLean

Fleeing her unfaithful fiancé, Lara sticks a pin in the map and vows to go wherever it lands. She finds herself in the cool summer of the Scottish Highlands, landing a job at Invermalloch Estate. Here, she meets Cal, the brooding Laird who is hiding from his own painful past. A powerful attraction between them slowly turns to love. But when Cal is called back to America, will this love survive — or will Lara's Highland Laird prove to be only a summer romance?